FORSWORN BY THE VAMPIRE

DEATHLESS NIGHT-INTO THE DARK #3

L.E. WILSON

EVERBLOOD
PUBLISHING

ALSO BY L.E. WILSON

Deathless Night Series (The Vampires)

A Vampire Bewitched

A Vampire's Vengeance

A Vampire Possessed

A Vampire Betrayed

A Vampire's Submission

A Vampire's Choice

Deathless Night-Into the Dark Series (The Vampires)

Night of the Vampire

Secret of the Vampire

Forsworn by the Vampire

The Kincaid Werewolves (The Werewolves)

Lone Wolf's Claim

A Wolf's Honor

The Alpha's Redemption

A Wolf's Promise

A Wolf's Treasure

The Alpha's Surrender

Southern Dragons (Dragon Shifters & Vampires)

Dance for the Dragon

Burn for the Dragon

<u>Snow Ridge Shifters (Novellas)</u>

A Second Chance on Snow Ridge

A Fake Fiancé on Snow Ridge

Copyright © 2021 by Everblood Publishing, LLC

All rights reserved. No part of this publication may be reproduced, distributed, or transmitted in any form or by any means, including photocopying, recording, or other electronic or mechanical methods, without the prior written permission of the publisher, except in the case of brief quotations embodied in critical reviews and certain other noncommercial uses permitted by copyright law. For permission requests, email the publisher, addressed "Attention: Permissions Coordinator," at the address below.

All characters and events in this book are fictitious. Any resemblance to actual persons – living or dead – is purely coincidental.

le@lewilsonauthor.com

ISBN: 978-1-945499-59-3

Print Edition

Publication Date: October 14, 2021

Copy Editor: Jinxie Gervasio @ jinxiesworld.com

Cover Design by Coffee and Characters

NOTE FROM THE AUTHOR

I mentioned this in the previous books, but I thought it was worth repeating...

If you are new to my books, there are a few things you need to know about this series to avoid any confusion.

The "Deathless Night-Into the Dark" series is an *extension* of the original "Deathless Night" series, picking up the storyline of The Moss Witches that was started in the original series. And, the characters from Deathless Night will be making appearances throughout this series. I'm thrilled to be with these characters again, and I hope you are, too!

Happy reading!

1

JAMAL

Tonight was the night I would leave.

I repeated this to myself over and over as I walked out of The Purple Fang, the male strip club my coven owned on Bourbon Street in The French Quarter of New Orleans. It was where we performed, and also where we fed. And the only place I felt like I didn't belong to anyone but myself.

It hadn't been my choice to work there. We were forced into the club by the restrictions of the witches. However, taking off my clothes for an audience was my choice. The women I gave special attention to in the back room were my choice. And the women I fed from and sometimes fucked were my choice.

Not anyone else's. MINE.

I pulled up the collar of my jacket to keep the wind off the back of my neck as I checked out the vibe outside the club. Things could get a little dicey in this part of the city at night, and it was always good to know what I was about to walk into. Wouldn't want to get caught by surprise and vamp out on somebody by accident. That always caused all kinds of problems. Girls screaming. Dudes pissing their pants. People getting trampled. And it was hard to catch everyone who saw what happened so we could make them forget. Then we had to bring the witches in, and they never failed to give us shit about it.

Girls who'd traded their bras for beads after too many Hurricanes and now couldn't find their hotel? I was more than happy to help get them there safe and sound in exchange for a tiny sip of that sweet blood they would never remember. Guys who couldn't handle their alcohol and were chasing each other up and down the street with busted beer bottles? Yeah, nah. Imma be getting the hell out of there quick. Let the cops handle those idiots.

It had started raining sometime earlier this afternoon, so Bourbon Street was relatively empty. And I was glad for it because I didn't bring the car. At least with no one around I didn't have to pretend to be human. I'd be home before the rain had a chance to soak my clothes. I could pack some stuff and be out of there before Killian had a chance to stop me. Because that's exactly what he would do. He wouldn't be able to help himself, no matter how much I told him I needed to go. And that's the only reason I had to sneak out without saying goodbye to him and the other four vampires I'd spent so many decades with. But he left me no choice.

And if I timed it just right, I could be in a completely new place by Christmas.

I started home, but I'd only gone about two blocks when I remembered I'd told Lizzy--Killian's new mate--I would stop by her shop for her. She'd left her dog's medication there, and rather than have her run out in the cold rain to get it, I told her I would stop on my way home since Killian was going to be stuck at the club for a while yet. My last good deed.

I liked Lizzy, and I liked her dog, Wiggles, and not only because she kept Killian off my back most of the time. It was just nice having another woman in the house. Good to come home and have the house smell like whatever she'd cooked for dinner. I couldn't eat it, but it was still nice. And she was an easy person to be around. She made it comfortable there. Homey. So, for her, I'd trek an extra few blocks out of my way, and even get my clothes wet.

About half a block from Lizzy's store, Ancient Magicks, I slowed down, narrowing my eyes. With my dark skin and clothes, it was easy for me to step into the entrance to a courtyard and not be noticed. Someone had just come out the door, the tinkling of the bell over the door coming to me easily down the empty street. The person's back was to me, and all I could tell was that it was a woman. Human. Her scent tickled my nose, made stronger by the humidity in the air. With a wave of her hand, she locked the door again--or so I assumed--looked up and down the street, and walked away, her hands shoved in her pockets and her bright red hair mostly covered with the hood of her black raincoat.

A witch. I knew that red hair, bright as a candied apple against her pale, white skin, reminding me of Leeloo in *The Fifth Element*. One of my favorite movies. As I watched her walk away, I let the witch put some distance between us as memories flashed through my head, one after the other.

Angel, that was her name. Angel Moss. One of the witches from the local coven run by Judy, Lizzy's aunt. I'd seen her around here and there over the last few years, but my most recent memory was from the night we'd all been here at the shop as they cast a spell to try to find Kenya, my best friend in the coven, after she'd disappeared on us. My stomach clenched as I remembered that night. It was something I'd rather try to forget. Like, for real.

When she was a good three blocks away from me, I started to follow her, curious as to what she was doing in there this late. I hadn't seen anything in her hands, but that didn't mean anything. She was a witch. She could hide shit easily. A fucking elephant could be strolling alongside her and I would never know it if she didn't want me to.

That kind of shit creeped out some vampires, and I was one hundred and fifty percent one of those bloodsuckers. It was strange, because I grew up with women--and some men-- practicing voodoo they'd brought with them from Haiti when they were forced to relocate to this country. But what the witches here practiced was nothing like voodoo. Nah. *That* shit was a different beast entirely. And it made my skin crawl like roaches were embedded in the muscle beneath it.

Angel stopped suddenly in the middle of the sidewalk, her head turning slightly, like she was listening to something. I ducked into a doorway, my own sensitive ears attuned to the night, but I heard nothing but the rain hitting the pavement and my own soft breathing. Did she sense me here somehow? I waited for her to turn around and look right at me, but she didn't. After a few heartbeats, she crossed the street and headed toward the Garden District. I wondered why she hadn't brought her car. It was a bit of a trek from our hood to hers on a cold, rainy night.

A few seconds later, I followed her, knowing I may not find out anything if she crossed into her neighborhood. It was warded by the witches. They would know as soon as I stepped foot over the line, and then there would be more questions than I was ready to answer. She walked two more blocks and turned a corner. Looking around to make sure there were no witnesses, I jogged ahead at vamp speed, slowing down only when I'd reached the street she'd turned on. I waited a heartbeat, and then leaned out around the corner. But she was fucking gone.

I walked around the corner, narrowing my eyes against the rain, but I couldn't find her anywhere. There was no way she'd made it to the next turn that fast. So she'd either gone inside one of these houses, or she'd known I was following her the entire time. "Dammit," I muttered.

"Why are you following me, vampire?"

I whipped around with a curse to find her directly behind me, hands in the pockets of her rain jacket, head tilted with curiosity.

"Hey, Leeloo."

She didn't bother to correct me, even though I knew the nickname irked her, which is why I used it. Instead, she just stood there, waiting for an explanation.

"What are you doing sneaking around Lizzy's shop?" I didn't know the extent of her magic, but from the way my skin tingled, and how my immediate instinct was to run as fast and far as I could, I figured it was safe to assume she was one of the more powerful ones. So I figured lying probably wasn't my best option here. That left me with avoidance.

To my surprise, she didn't push it. "None of your business." She went to walk around me, and without thinking I grabbed her elbow to stop her.

A current of energy whipped up my arm, zapping me like I'd just licked a live electrical wire, and I jerked back, releasing my hold on her and throwing my hands in front of me, palms out. Baring my teeth as the hair rose on the back of my neck, I muttered, "Sorry, princess."

"Don't flash your fangs at me, vampire. I'm not afraid of your bite."

My cock twitched in my pants as I wondered if her blood was as spicy as her personality. "Keep your fucking magic in check, Leeloo. I just wanna talk."

"There's nothing for us to discuss," she told me. "I was in the shop. The shop once owned by our coven and still owned by my cousin, who will be a full member as soon as she stops trying to deny her heritage. It's none of your concern why I was there or what I was doing. End of discussion. Now stop following me."

She turned to leave, and I reached out to stop her again before I remembered myself and rushed around her to block her path instead. She stopped when I appeared in front of her, her face a mask of impatience, but she didn't try to go around me or zap me out of her way. She didn't even startle when I suddenly showed up there. "I'm getting wet," she said in a bored voice.

I knew what she meant, and still my mind immediately went there. A low growl rose in my chest, but I bit it off before she could hear it. My nostrils flared, searching for more of her scent. Mmmm...there it was. Earthy and sweet and full of spice, just as I remembered. It made my mouth water.

"If you have something to say, say it. Otherwise get the hell out of my way."

"Jamal," I told her.

"What?"

"My name is Jamal."

She lifted one dark eyebrow, as if to say, "And?"

"Does Lizzy know you were in her shop?"

"Good gods, vampire, drop it already, will you? You've got nothing on me."

I fought the smirk at her refusal to call me by my name. "Then why won't you tell me what you were doing there?"

"What were *you* doing there?" she asked me.

"What?"

"'Turnaround is fair play, right? You tell me what you were doing there and I'll tell you why I was there."

"I was getting Wiggles' medication that Lizzy accidentally left there when she locked up earlier today." Crossing my arms over my chest, I waited for her reciprocate.

The rain started to come down harder, and she gave the sky a dirty look and then pulled her hood down farther over her face. "It was nice chatting with you, Jamal," she dragged my name out, "but I gotta go." She took a step toward me, so close I could feel her body heat through the raincoat she was wearing. I stared down into her hazel eyes, moss green with streaks of golden brown, then dipped down to her ruby red lips, watching as her tongue wet her the bottom one, adding to the sheen of her lipstick. "If I stay here with you any longer," she purred, "I'm going to be completely drenched." She looked up at me, the corners of her mouth turning up into a feline smile.

I stood there, unable to move, my heart pounding and my cock hard as she walked around me and crossed the border into The Garden District.

2

ANGEL

Fuck. Fuck. Fuck.

What the hell was that vampire doing snooping around The Quarter at two in the morning? Shouldn't he be taking advantage of some innocent woman in the back of their club or feeding on her angry husband or something?

Taking a deep breath, I glanced back over my shoulder. I knew he wasn't following me anymore, but I could still feel the weight of his stare on my back. Or maybe some small part of me who liked to live dangerously was just hoping he would ignore the spelled border...

But no, there he stood, looking like some kind of goddamn biker magazine ad with the collar of his black, leather jacket up around his neck, the rain glistening on his dark brown skin like tiny diamonds, perfectly illuminated by the streetlight above him.

I'd never noticed how light his eyes are before. More topaz than brown.

With a huff of impatience aimed more at myself than at him, I whipped my head back around and kept walking.

Fucking vampires. Always sticking their noses in our business. And now I was on his radar, and something about the way he was watching me told me I wouldn't be coming off of it anytime soon.

I shoved down the panic that was bubbling up inside of me. There was no way he knew what I was really doing at Lizzy's shop. He had nothing on me.

Still, I opened my chakras and sent out a pulse of magic, testing the wards placed around The Garden District where I lived. The spell wasn't made to keep the vampires out, but it did let us know whenever one came into our neighborhood. Our relationship with our supernatural neighbors was much less strained these days since two of our own mated with two of theirs, but it still didn't hurt to be cautious.

I didn't breathe easy again until I was about two blocks from my apartment. Maybe "easy" wasn't the right word. But at least I didn't feel like my heart was about to explode from my chest, something I'd immediately hid behind a quick spell so the vampire wouldn't hear it. He knew better than to think I was scared of him, so he would correctly assume that I was hiding something. And he was already suspicious enough.

As I got to the front door of my apartment, I glanced back one more time, listening for anything from the boundary spell that would tell me it had been crossed.

But all was still and silent. Slipping inside, I took the stairs up to the third floor and went directly to my place.

The door was flung open before I could insert my key all the way into the lock. "Where the fuck have you been, Angel?"

"Trying to save your ass, Mike. That's where I've been."

My best friend looked like I had the one time I'd found myself in the throes of a bad break-up. There was only that once, though, because that was the last time I'd let anyone get that close to me. His hair--red like mine on top (because I'd had extra color and he'd had too much to drink) and bleached on the sides--looked like he'd been tugging on it all night, and his lean, muscular body was hidden beneath my blanket robe.

I made a face. "Are you wearing anything under there?"

He just stared at me with eyes as clear and blue as a tropical sea. Didn't so much as raise an eyebrow.

Shoving him out of the doorway, I pushed past him and closed the door. "I went by the shop to see if I could find something that could possibly get you out of this mess I'd gotten you into."

Mike leaned back against the closed door and watched me move around the small kitchen, making some orange spice tea. It was late, and I was tired, but restless. Tea would help.

"What could Lizzy possibly have in that tourist shop that would catch the interest of a djinn?" he asked. "I work there, Ang. There's nothing there but fake voodoo shit and beads."

"I don't appreciate the tone," I responded.

He cocked his head to the side, a smirk teasing his lips and his eyes full of amusement at my expense.

I stuck my cup under the one cup coffee maker and hit the button for hot water only, then I turned around, leaning against the counter, and crossed my arms over my chest. I eyed him a minute, and then, with a sigh, I reached into the waistline of my pants at my back and pulled out a dagger. Without a word, I laid it on the counter beside me.

"THAT was not in Lizzy's store." He pointed at the ancient looking relic. "What is that?" he asked.

"A knife," I told him.

"No shit, Ang. What are you planning to do with it?"

I glanced down at the "knife". It needed to be cleaned, but I could still see the faint lines of the runes carved into the blade. "I'm going to use it to kill the djinn. After I tweak it a bit with a spell."

"What kind of a spell?"

Sighing heavily, I turned around to get my tea. "The kind that will help me kill a djinn, Mike. For fuck's sake."

"Snapping at me is not necessary," he declared. "Jesus, I'm just asking."

I glanced over my shoulder at him, then took a deep breath as I dunked my teabag a few times. "You're right." I paused. "I'm sorry. And thanks for not hating me," I told him. "Ya know...for getting the both of us into all of this shit."

Opening the blanket robe, he brought it up over his head, revealing a hard, bare chest and pajama bottoms before he wrapped it tight around himself again. "I do hate you, Ang. However, you're the only friend I have right now who understands why I am the way I am after being the made into the plaything of a djinn."

"You make it sound like he demanded sexual favors from you."

"It wouldn't have surprised me," he countered. "But lucky for you, he only made me sit here with his magical fist around my heart until you made sure he got away free and clear. Do you know how fucking terrifying that was? Feeling my heart squeeze inside of my chest every time you mouthed off to him?" He paused. "At least I assume that's what you were doing."

I wouldn't look at him. He knew me too well.

"What's wrong with you? Why are you so quiet?"

I shrugged. "Nothing. It's been a long day." I knew better than to think he'd let it go at that, but a girl could hope, right?

"Ang." There was a warning in his tone that told me my assumption had been correct.

Picking up my teacup, I held it in both hands and turned around to face him. "It's really nothing. One of the vampires saw me coming out of the shop and followed me for a bit, that's all. I handled it."

"Which one?"

"The scary one that never smiles."

"Jamal," Mike said immediately.

"I guess so." I kept my voice casual, playing it off like I didn't know *exactly* who he was, and had ever since the first time I saw him.

"Fuck."

"That's exactly what I said." I took a sip of my tea, made a face, and set it back on the counter. Then I grabbed some honey out of the cabinet and drizzled some into my cup. "But like I said, I handled it." And I was a fool to believe he didn't suspect anything.

That vampire--Jamal--he wasn't going to let me play this off as just two people who happened to both be wandering The Quarter in the middle of the night in rain cold enough to even keep the tourists off the streets. I knew that the moment our eyes had met.

I'd seen him around before, of course, but I'd never really had any interaction with him until the night we'd all gathered in the shop to do a location spell when we'd lost Alex and Kenya. His golden eyes had been black with worry for his friend as he'd prowled around the store like an animal trapped in a cage. With his energy level running so high, it had been hard for me and the rest of the witches to concentrate on what we were doing: the coven trying to find

Alex and Kenya, and me, trying to sabotage the spell from the inside so it would show them the wrong location. Something that was hard as all hell to do for a simple witch but shouldn't have been that hard for me.

"How exactly did you handle it?" Mike asked. "Please tell me you didn't do anything stupid."

"Of course not. I just told him it was none of his business."

The eyebrow was back. "And he just let you go."

"Stop with the fucking tone," I warned him.

As a powerless human male, he should've been afraid. However, Mike wasn't afraid of very much. Except perhaps a djinn. And a cold draft apparently. "You're so fucked."

"I know," I said softly, then took a sip of my tea.

3

JAMAL

When I got home the big house was dark. Everyone else was still at the club except for Lizzy, who still worked during the day and hadn't yet adapted to our schedule. Although as the owner of a voodoo store, I thought it would be perfectly appropriate to have that bitch open at night. But she claimed once the sun started to set, everyone was too drunk to let them loose in her shop.

In any case, it wasn't my problem. Pushing all thoughts of Lizzy, the redhead, and whatever dirty business she was up to out of my mind, I checked the time on my phone. I had six hours until the sun came up. Probably one or two before everyone else started wandering in. Plenty of time to pack some things and get as far from here as I could. By the time the sun set, I'd have a good head start. They might search for me for a bit, but hopefully, in the end, Killian will realize that the best thing he can do for me is to let me go. Let me be free.

I rubbed my hands over my skull, trying to calm my nerves that had sprung up out of nowhere. I'd tried to leave before, once right after Killian had turned me, and again about fifty years ago. Both times Killian had hunted me down, and I'd come back, guilted into it by the blood bond between us and his relentless need to hoard anything he considered his, including people and vampires. He was going to lose his shit when he found out I really did it this time. I dropped my hands to my face, then let my arms fall to my sides. The thought didn't make me feel better about my decision. We'd been together a long time. But this time, he had Lizzy. And I was hoping his mating with her would allow him to break the bond with me.

I fucking hated Killian for making me into the thing I now was.

I also loved him more than I'd ever loved anyone, except maybe my mother.

He'd saved my life, not once, but twice. The first time was shortly after he'd helped me get free from the white slave owner who'd purchased my parents. The second time, it had cost me that freedom I'd fought so fucking hard for. Because the second time, he'd made me into the creature I am now, and <u>he</u> became my master. He'd kept me alive when I wanted to throw myself into the sun. He taught me to hunt. Taught me how to control my hunger. And stuck with me through the severe mood swings new vampires go through. Spinning round and round like a roulette wheel, never knowing where I was going to end up or who this new me would be.

And when I finally did stop, I was angry. Fucking pissed that he'd made me into a vampire like him. That he hadn't given me a choice.

I was born into slavery. And after only a few years of being my own man, owned by no one, I was once again a slave to the master vampire who clung to me out of his own desperate need for a family. And still wouldn't let me go.

This time, however, this time would be different. Killian had Lizzy, his mate. He wouldn't leave her to come after me. He was too fucking possessive for that. He had a hard enough time letting her go to her shop every day, especially since Mike had disappeared and she was there by herself. Alone. During the daylight hours when he couldn't get to her if something happened. It drove him absolutely fucking insane, though he tried not to show her that.

Kicking off my sneakers so I didn't track whatever filth the rain had dredged up from the sidewalks inside, I set the dog's meds on the kitchen counter where Lizzy would easily be able to find them. Then I stood there in the dark, looking around the place.

I would miss this house.

And I would miss the people in it, both vampire and human.

I debated waking up Lizzy to say goodbye. I think she would understand why I needed to go and not try to stop me. But she might also tell Killian I'd left before I was ready for him to know I was gone.

Taking a deep breath, I walked over to the back door and slid my shoes back on. For as much time as I spent here, this wasn't my home. I stayed in the little guest house out back by choice. Killian had suggested it when we moved in here to give me--what he termed--a little more space and independence. And I'd agreed so that when I decided to leave, it would be easier.

Inside my place, I left the sliding door open that led into the kitchen and went straight to my room to pack my things, not caring what I tracked across the tile floor. I didn't have much. Just some clothes. A toothbrush. Nothing that would remind me of this place. I wasn't into keepsakes. What was the point? So you could sit around staring at them feeling sad that you weren't there anymore? No thanks. I'd spent my entire life trying to forget the places I'd come from. There was nothing here I wanted to remember.

A woman's face drifted through my mind. Hazel-green eyes and red lips surrounded by cherry-red hair. "Leeloo" I'd called her. But that wasn't really right. In *The Fifth Element*, Milla Jovovich's hair was more of an orange. Not such a deep red. Same kind of cut though, so close enough as far as I was concerned.

I hadn't been able to find anything amiss in Lizzy's shop when I'd gotten there. Everything seemed to be in place. Nothing missing as far as I could tell. I'd even gone into the back room and moved the shelf away from the door that led into the witch's secret meeting room, but I couldn't get it open. It must be spelled shut or some shit.

I stilled, my hands full of shirts.

What if that was it? What if the witch wasn't trying to steal something? What if she was leaving something there? A spell. Or some sort of magical object. Something that could hurt Lizzy or Wiggles? And I was the only one who'd seen her do it?

I could leave Lizzy a note. But I immediately discarded that idea. For one, it would tip off both her and Killian that I'd left. And I wanted to put some more distance between me and them, just in case I was wrong and he did come after me. And two, what the hell was I supposed to tell them? One of your cousins was sneaking out of your store at 2am but she didn't take anything or do any other harm as far as I could tell but she was acting suspicious as all hell?

That sounded stupid, even to me.

Know what? Not my problem. I continued packing. Whatever Angel was up to with the witches wasn't anything I needed to be sticking my nose into. I never should've followed her to begin with. Restrictions between the covens had eased up a bit after what happened with Kenya and Alex, and although the witches still kept their neighborhood warded to sense intruders, we could go there whenever we wanted. And they could come here to The Quarter. It wasn't a big deal.

So why were my spidey senses going off?

Something was going on with that witch, Angel. I could feel it in my bones. And if it was just her, I'd walk away without a backward glance.

Liar. You're wouldn't walk away from her. Not now. Face it, man. You're involved.

Fuck. Maybe that was true. Maybe I wouldn't. But it was only because I'd grown up the way I had, and I sensed a kindred spirit in her. Not that she'd been born to pick cotton until the sun roasted the skin from your bones and you could barely make it to your lumpy cot, where you shoved some gruel down your throat and fell into an exhausted sleep and prayed you wouldn't wake up the next morning. But there was something about her that told me she felt just as stuck as I did. Just as used. Just as silenced.

Still, I didn't care about her. But I did care about Lizzy, and that woman had never been anything but kind to me. Also, she was Killian's, which meant, for now, she was also mine, and I should do whatever I had to do to protect her.

It had absolutely nothing to do with a witch who let me follow her home, only to tease me with her innuendos until my cock swelled to an uncomfortable size inside my jeans.

With a sound of disgust aimed directly at myself, I set down my bag and began to unpack.

4

ANGEL

"Where are you going?"

Mike stopped with one hand on the front door knob. "Are you kidding me right now, Ang? I'm getting the fuck out of here. I'm sorry. I love you. You know I do. But I'm so done with all of this magic shit." He paused. "I am really sorry," he said, a bit calmer now but just as determined. "But I think leaving the city is the best thing I can do right now. I don't want to be anywhere near you or that thing you summoned."

"I get that. I do. But please trust me when I tell you this is the safest place for you."

He gave me a look that let me know exactly how much he didn't believe me.

"Besides," I told him. "I doesn't matter if you're here in New Orleans or not. If the djinn wants to find you, he will, no matter where you go."

Mike's hand fell from the knob and he dropped his duffel bag containing his clothes and things he'd brought with him when he'd shown up at her door. The anger was back. "Fuck me, Ang. You've totally fucked me. And not in a good way." With jerky movements, he took off his coat and threw it on the floor, then stomped over to the couch and sat down.

"I'm trying to fix it."

He wouldn't look at me as he hung his coat on the hanger just inside the door.

"Michael. I'm *going* to fix it."

Eyes still on the floor, he gave me a nod and walked past me to go back to the couch. Picking up the remote, he turned on the television and pulled the comforter around him that he'd left there. "I just want to go back to work with Lizzy at her voodoo store without worrying about dropping dead in the middle of a sale. Maybe grab a beer with the guys and not have my heart explode in my chest. Is that too much to fucking ask?"

I walked over and sat on the coffee table in front of him, forcing him to look at me. "I will get you out of this. I've thought of something the djinn wants. Something that I can deliver to him."

"What's that?"

"Witches. He wants witches on his side. And..." I paused, taking a breath, because the moment I said the words I would have to carry through with it, "I can give him that. I can give him me."

Mike's eyes shot to mine. "What are you talking about? He already has you."

I shook my head. "Only in a limited capacity. I'm going to offer him my life's services. And maybe I can even get Alice on his side." Too nervous to sit, I stood up and began to pace back and forth in front of the TV. "Alex is a lost cause, now that he's mated to Kenya. Especially not after what the djinn did to them. But maybe Alice...she *is* his niece. Then again, she's also very loyal to the coven, and Judy in particular."

"Judy is a good High Priestess, from what you've told me."

"She is," I agreed grudgingly. But she wasn't as good as she could be. She was too protective of us. Made it impossible for us to become as strong as we could be if she would let us push ourselves and our magic.

But Mike was already shaking his head. "No, Ang. You can't do that. That's a life sentence. He'll never let you go."

"I have to," I told him. "I have to finish what I began."

Mike sat foreword on the couch, his head in his hands. When he looked up again, his hair was sticking up all over his head in a sexy kind of bedhead. Not for the first time, I wished he was more my type. In normal circumstances, and hell, even in the worst ones, Mike was a sweet guy. He never screamed at me. Never raised a hand to me. Of course, that could be because he was afraid of me. Well, afraid of my magic. But we got along great. And I knew he wanted to fuck me. And in better times, we spent most of our time flirting with each other.

But alas, we were destined to just be friends.

I started gathering what I needed to take with me. "I'll be back in a few days. Maybe a week." Slinging my backpack over my shoulder, I checked that I had my keys and my wallet.

"Wait. Where are YOU going?" He ran his eyes over me, like he was just now noticing the clothes I was wearing. Jeans, a hoodie, and running shoes. Very dressed down compared to what I usually liked to wear. But I couldn't very well fight a djinn in heels and a feathery top. Besides, where I was going, no one was going to see me.

"I have to take care of this." I gave him a smile. "Stay here though, okay? This place is warded against intruders. You'll be safe here."

"Will it keep the djinn out?"

"No," I told him after a pause. "But it will let me know if he's here. And I'll be able to get help to you as fast as possible. Just try to stay alive till then."

Jumping up off the couch, Mike came to stand in front of me, his expression serious. "Seriously, Ang. Where are you going?"

"It's better if you don't know," I told him. "Not because I don't trust you, but because if you don't know, you can't be forced to tell."

He stared at me for a long time, his eyes roaming over my features. Then he cupped my face between his hands and leaned down to kiss me. A real kiss. Not the playful pecks he usually gave me.

It was strange, kissing Mike. Not unpleasant. But not exactly fireworks, either. And it wasn't because he wasn't a good-looking guy. He was. Mike was slender, but he was all muscle. And he had a face that reminded me of Zac Efron, only better. He was fun, and sweet, he showered regularly, and loved to hang out with me. He was everything a girl could want. Hell, he'd even dyed his hair to match mine, adding his own flair with the blonde. But there was just...nothing. At least not on my part. But that wasn't anything we needed to get into right now.

"Be careful," he told me when he broke off the kiss.

"I will," I promised. With another quick kiss on his cheek, I walked out the door.

5

JAMAL

"Have any of you guys seen Angel by chance?" Lizzy asked when she got home.

"Which one is she again?" Dae asked.

"The redhead," I told him.

"Ohhhh...*that* one."

I'd been about to ask Lizzy why she was asking, but something about Dae's tone got under my skin. "What the hell is that supposed to mean?" I felt Killian's eyes on me from across the room, the book he'd been reading lowering to his lap as he studied me.

Just then, the dryer sang its little song, telling us the laundry was done. "She's hot," Dae said over his shoulder as he went to go get his clothes. "'That's all."

A growl rumbled low in my throat, and I looked up to find Lizzy giving me an odd look. Before she could start asking me any questions, I got up and left the room, heading out the back door to go back to the guest house.

The guest house. Even the name of where I lived implied I was nothing but a temporary resident.

"Jamal, wait!"

I stopped, but didn't turn. The back door slammed shut, and a few seconds later, I felt Lizzy's hand on my arm. She peeked around my shoulder, her brow furrowed with concern. "What's going on with you?"

"Nothing I want to talk about," I told her, not unkindly.

She studied me a moment, but didn't push it. "Do you know where Angel is, by chance?"

"Why would I know that?"

Stepping in front of me so she could face me full on, she wrapped her arms around herself, shivering. I guess it would be cold for her. I hadn't really noticed. "We're afraid something may have happened. No one has heard from her since yesterday, not even Mike, who actually deigned to answer his phone this time. And still won't tell me where he is on this sudden 'vacation' of his..." Her expression became thoughtful.

A burning sensation erupted in my chest at the mention of that little punk's name, but I pushed it aside, focusing on what was important and not my dislike for Lizzy's assistant. And certainly not because every time I saw him aside from

Ancient Magicks he was always hanging around with a certain, redheaded witch. "Can't you guys just do one of those location spells and find her?" I didn't know why she was telling me all of this. Angel Moss was not my problem.

Lizzy looked down at her feet, and I saw her shoulders rise and fall on a deep sigh. I narrowed my eyes at the top of her dark head. I knew what she was doing. And it wasn't going to work.

But she surprised me. Instead of trying to wheedle what she wanted out of me, when she looked up, her jaw was set in that stubborn way she had when she was determined to get her way. "Look," she told me. "You can live in denial all you want, but I know there's something between the two of you. I saw it that day at the shop when we were all there."

"There's absolutely nothing between me and that witch."

She continued on as if I hadn't spoken. "We can't find her, Jamal. No one has heard from her. Not even Mike. And those two are practically inseparable lately. Not that I think there's anything romantic there," she was quick to point out. Then she sighed. "Any spell we try is blocked. We're afraid she's in some kind of trouble."

"Did you try her house? Or apartment? Or wherever she lives?" It inexplicably bothered me that I didn't even know that much about her.

Lizzy nodded. "Of course. That was the first place we checked. I ran over with Aunt Judy yesterday. No one was there."

"Maybe she just wanted some alone time. She doesn't seem the type to need a babysitter."

"She doesn't," Lizzy agreed. "But as thorny and spontaneous as she can be, she's never just disappeared like this. Not without telling someone." She ran her eyes over my face, searching for some hint that I cared, maybe? "Jamal, I know you know something we don't. And I know it has to do with Angel. I don't know how I know that, but I do. I can feel it every time you're around me. All I'm asking is that you tell me so we can try to find her."

I stared at her, but said nothing. Damn witches and their sixth senses. Of course, with Lizzy, it might be more than that. She was still getting to know her magic after a life of being in denial of who and what she is.

"Jamal, please. I'm really worried. Something's wrong. I can feel it in my bones. We all can."

"I thought you didn't like her."

"I don't. She's a complete bitch to me, but that doesn't mean I want something to happen to her. Bitch or not, she's still family."

Running my hand over my shaved skull and down to the back of my neck, I tried to ease some of the tension there. "Look, Liz. I'd love to help you, but I really don't know where she is or what she might be doing." That was true. "I barely speak to the woman." Also true. "And I'm supposed to be at the club in a few hours, so I don't know how much help I can be. Besides, she's got a whole coven of witches looking out for her, I'm sure they'll find her before either of us could."

"They all went to Seattle for a meeting with the coven up there," she said distractedly. "Angel was left here to keep an eye on things. I haven't heard from her since." She chewed on her thumbnail for a few seconds. "So you haven't seen her recently? Are you sure?"

Jesus fuck. I couldn't lie to her. "Just briefly on the street the other night when she was wandering around The Quarter."

She perked up at that. "Did you talk to her?"

"Again, just briefly. I have no idea what she was doing, but she seemed to be heading home. That's all I know. I'm sorry." All true. I don't know why I felt the need to leave out some parts, other than I felt like somehow I would be betraying Angel's trust to say more.

She stared at me for a long time, like she thought if she did it long enough, she'd eventually see through to whatever she thought I was hiding from her. Finally, she dropped her eyes. Without a word, she walked around me and back into the main house.

"I'm sure she's fine!" I called after her. "Fuck." I released a deep breath through my mouth and continued on my way. But even after I got inside, I couldn't settle down. All I kept seeing was Lizzy's brown eyes, filled with worry and disappointment in me. What if she was right? What if Angel was in trouble? That girl was definitely up to something. Maybe I should've told Lizzy that I saw her sneaking out of her shop the other night. What if she got herself into some type of a mess she couldn't get out of? And what if Lizzy got pulled into it?

I stopped pacing my small kitchen and stared out the sliding doors toward the big house, different scenarios tumbling around in my head, and not a damn one of them good. Then I gave myself a hard internal shake. Nah. I was letting Lizzy get to me. Dae was right. Angel was hot. And stuff could happen. But she was also a witch. No one in this city could do anything to her that she didn't want them to do. Not even someone like me.

But what if it wasn't someone like us?

What if it wasn't a some*one* at all, but a some*thing*?

After Kenya's attempted kidnapping, we never did figure out how the hell the djinn had escaped, not as injured as he was. That warlock--the scary one with the bird...Jesse--swore he'd exhausted enough of his magic that the only way he would've been able to get out of the city was if he'd had help. So, where had he gone? We'd all searched the woods surrounding the swamp house until the sun had forced us back to The Quarter. We'd found nothing...

Except some tire tracks.

However, we'd never found the car they belonged to. And no one recalled seeing or hearing anything. But magic could easily cover that. So, why didn't the djinn and whoever his little helper was make those tracks disappear? It's almost like they wanted to get caught.

I started pacing again as some seriously fucked up thoughts ran through my mind. But then I shook my head. Nah. She wouldn't be stupid enough to get involved with something like that. The cost would be too great. Djinns were notorious for their crafty ways. Angel would know better than to get involved with him.

Unless he was holding something over her.

My guts began to churn, and I made a beeline for the bathroom, splashing cold water on my face. The djinn were nothing to fuck with. Hell, even I knew that. Surely, Angel did, too.

Grabbing the hand towel, I dried my face, then left it lying on the small counter as I argued with myself. It couldn't be true. Lizzy just had me all fucking paranoid. Sure, I'd caught Angel sneaking around. And yeah, she was snippy with her answers. But why shouldn't she be? She didn't owe me anything. Hell, she barely knew me.

But...but. What if I was right? What if she was in some kind of trouble?

With a muttered oath, I got my coat out of the closet and slammed out of the house. "Fucking witches and their fucking problems. It's none of my fucking business, so why are they getting me involved?" Glancing up at the main house, I saw Lizzy at the side window. When she noticed me leaving, she ran to the back door...

But I was already gone.

6

JESSE

Seattle, WA

I sat on a bench, my body angled so I was facing my sister. We were in a park in the middle of Seattle, bundled up against the cold. But it was a rare sunny day for this late in the year, and I'd talked her into coming out here with me for a while before the sunset, away from the eyes and ears of the others. "Ryan, you'll never be able to live a normal life if you don't learn how to control the voices."

"You mean I just have to show them who's boss?" A small smile flirted about her lips, and I found myself smiling back.

Separated from her since birth, getting to know her now has been a highlight of my life, right below meeting my Shea, yet she wasn't quite comfortable with me yet. Not like she was with the other witches. This was why even something as seemingly insignificant as a poor excuse for a joke and a shy smile caused joy to bloom in my chest.

"Something like that," I told her. "They'll listen to you if you stop being afraid of them and trying to push them away. If you can learn how to make them do your bidding, instead of just allowing yourself to hear them until they get out of hand, and then shutting them out again." By drinking her mate's vampire blood. At least it was better than the injections of opioids she used before she met him, and honestly, I didn't know how long it would continue to work for her. Would she develop a resistance to the effects? It was better for her to be prepared. "If you can master this, you can master anything. You'll be almost as scary as I am," I teased with a devilish smirk.

She glanced over at me, tucking a strand of bright red hair behind her ear. "How do you know that?"

"Because I can sense the power within you. You're stronger than anyone here, other than myself. Even Keira."

A woman and her dog walked by, a giant fluff of a thing, and Ryan gave them her attention, her expression and posture relaxed. But I could hear the fear and confusion in her mind. "The spirits, they really just want to help you, Ryan."

"Not all of them," she said without looking at me. "I heard about you and your demons in your mountain altar room."

"No, you're right," I said. "They didn't want to help me. They're demons." It was an offhand comment, but I didn't miss the stiffening of her shoulders by my saying the name so casually. "But they still did, because I'm more powerful than something that has no physical form. Just like you are. The spirits around you, my sister, they can work for you. If you'll let them."

The dog and its owner took a bend on the trail and walked out of sight. Leaning back on the bench, I tilted my head back, enjoying the subtle warmth of the winter sun as I gave her time to mull it all over. It wasn't anything she hadn't heard before, more or less, and not just from me, but the other witches, too. Yet, my sister remained resistant. I wasn't quite sure what the cause was, or how to convince her otherwise, and I was hoping by having some alone time with her I'd be able to get to the root of it.

Because I was going to need her help to kill our father.

As though she'd read my mind, a power I possessed but wasn't at all certain my sister was capable of, she asked, "Are you really going to do it? Kill the djinn?"

She refused to call him "father", but then again, she'd never known him. Hell, the word often stuck in my own throat. "I am," I told her with certainty. Because there was no doubt in my mind.

"Why kill him?" she still wouldn't look at me. Instead, she glanced around nervously, and with her next words, I knew exactly what she was worried about without having to delve into her mind. "Why not just...send him away?"

"They won't tell him, if that's what you're worried about. The spirits," I clarified. "They won't tell him."

Finally, her blue eyes met mine. It never ceased to surprise me, when she looked at me like this, how much she looked like our mother. "You're sure?"

"Yes. And even if they did, I would never allow him to hurt you. Or any of us." My tone and volume didn't change. I didn't need it to.

She stuck her hands deeper into her pockets and shivered. "Okay."

"We can go back if you're too cold," I offered.

"No," she said without hesitation. "Not just yet."

I was used to hiding my emotions. I'd gotten so good at it over the years that not so much as my heartbeat would give me away. It was a protective measure I'd had to master living amongst vampires who wouldn't hesitate to rip me apart in my sleep if I gave them the slightest cause to think they could possibly overcome me. However, first around my Shea...and now my sister...I found the feelings she provoked to be so profound it was impossible to quell my excitement that she trusted me enough to stay here with me. Not completely. And it was one of the reasons I wanted to be alone with her.

But I didn't want to overwhelm her, so I focused on the conversation and tried to explain. "I don't have the book to send him home to his own dimension, so killing him is the only choice I'm left with. He doesn't belong here in this world."

Ryan was quiet for a very long time. And then she turned to me again and asked, "Do we?"

I frowned. "Do we what?"

"Belong. In this world."

Her eyes, as blue as the sky above where Cruthú flew in circles above us, were full of uncertainty as she looked to me for the truth. There was no hesitation in my answer.

"Yes, sister. We do."

She stared at me for a long moment, studying my expression, searching for lies in my eyes, but she found nothing. "Okay," she said again. "Do you know where he is?"

"No." I paused, wondering how much I should tell her. But if I wanted her to put her trust in me as her brother, I would have to do the same. "That's not entirely true. I know where he is, I just can't find it."

"I don't understand."

"He's moved the mountain."

Ryan stared at me like perhaps she'd been too hasty in agreeing to come outside alone in the full light of day with someone who was clearly out of their mind.

"Let me explain before you judge me."

"I'm not judging you."

I cocked my head to the side and raised an eyebrow.

"I just wonder how sane you are," she admitted. "Like maybe you're talking to the invisible voices for entirely too long."

"Well, sister mine, if that's the reason I'm insane, then surely you're not very far behind."

"Hmph." But she smiled. "Okay, tell me how anyone could possibly move a mountain."

"With magic, of course. I don't know that he actually moved it, I just can't find it. And neither can anyone else. Not for at least thirty years."

"Then how will we find him?"

"We don't need to find him, we just need to find the book." I gave her a meaningful look.

"And that's why you need me to gain control of these fucking things that are constantly screaming in my ears if I let them."

"Exactly," I said, leaning my head back to search for Cruthú in the trees. Spotting her at the top of the tallest pine, keeping a close eye on anyone who should come anywhere near us, I told Ryan, "I'm absolutely positive my father has hidden it somewhere. He's too intelligent to keep it with him. It's too risky, because he knows damn well I'll destroy it when I find him. And I WILL find him. Eventually."

Her hand, the one closest to me, lifted from her lap and hovered in the air a moment. My breath froze in my lungs, but I forced myself to breathe. Not to make any sudden movements, other than to turn my own hand until it was palm up on my leg. And then I watched as she slowly and carefully placed her hand in mine. My heart swelled almost painfully, and I wrapped my fingers around hers.

She stared down at our hands for a few seconds. "I'll help you," she finally said.

"Thank you, sister."

We sat in silence, our hands clutched together on my thigh, as the sun fell below the horizon and the temperature dropped. I looked up, hoping to see stars, but the lights from this beautiful city obscured my view. When full darkness fell, I tugged her up and off the bench, and I held her hand all the way home, Cruthú swooping down to land on my shoulder as we approached the apartment building where the vampires--and now us--lived, and for the first time, I dreaded this war that was fast approaching. But we had company coming from New Orleans, and we had to tell them what we knew and prepare for what was to come.

It was time.

7

ANGEL

I'd been at the cemetery for three days when he found me.

I don't know how he did it. The tomb I was hiding in belonged to my family. It was sealed and warded. No one could get in there unless they knew how. Surrounded by the remains of my ancestors, I'd felt safe while I cast my spells, sleeping only in short spurts, sponge bathing instead of showering, and surviving on snack foods and bottled water.

When the tomb began to shake around me, I'd thought at first we were having an earthquake, or that the city had been hit by a tsunami. But it was neither of those things.

"Come out, witch. Or I'm coming in."

The djinn's voice echoed off the walls of the tomb as though he were standing right beside me. Picking up the dagger from the center of the circle of stones, I backed away from the candles.

"I know you're in there. I can smell the stench of those spells you're trying to cast."

Fuck. Fuck. Fuck! How the hell had Marcus found me? I tried to think. Tried to think what to do. Quickly, I put the dagger down the back of my pants beneath my hoodie. With a wave of my hand, the rocks scattered across the floor. Another wave and the flames on the candles extinguished themselves.

The ground rolled, rising and falling beneath my feet. I stumbled into the wall of the tomb as the door flew open.

With a look that would fell a normal man, I steadied myself and blew softly toward the torch on the wall beside my head, magically putting out the flame, then straightened off the wall and strolled out of the tomb, shutting the door behind me. Forcing my heart to calm its frantic beating, I faced the djinn full on.

"What are you doing in there?" he asked me.

"I needed some alone time," I told him flippantly. "What are *you* doing here? And why are you crashing into my private space?"

He stared at me long and hard, and I felt him digging around in my mind, trying to decipher the truth from my thoughts. But I was prepared, and he found nothing he didn't need to know. "I've been trying to call you."

Frowning, I pulled my cell out of my front pocket. There were no missed calls.

"Not that way," he said, his voice laced with disgust.

Oh. With magic. It couldn't get through the spells warding the tomb. "Sorry," I told him. "I must've been distracted." I slid my phone back into my pocket.

"You're lucky that was the only way I attempted to get your attention."

I knew he was talking about Mike. Anger roared through my blood unchecked before I could stop it. "Leave him out of this."

"But he's an essential part of 'this'." He smiled, his face handsome, like an actor from a classic movie with his dark hair cut into an old-fashioned style. But his good looks didn't hide the evil beneath. "As are you."

My fingers tingled as my magic danced beneath the surface of my skin. I clenched my hands into fists. This wasn't the time. I wasn't ready. But this might be the only chance I got. "I want Mike out of this arrangement between us. You don't need him."

"I disagree," the djinn told me. His eyes narrowed on my face, and my heart plummeted to my stomach. He knew I was up to something.

"Look, Marcus..." Just saying his name made me cringe inside. It was too personal. Too intimate. "I have a new offer for you."

A smile tugged at one side of his mouth. He thought he had me figured out. "Don't you want to hear why I'm here?"

"Not particularly, no." I was pushing my luck. However, terrified as I was, I still wasn't about to bow down to this son of a bitch. "Don't you want to hear *my* offer?"

Sliding his hands into the front pocket of his slacks, he glanced up at the darkening sky. There were no orange and pink streaks as the sun set this time of year. Only clouds and dropping temperatures that made me shiver beneath my layers of clothes. When he looked back at me, I held his gaze with my own. "Oh, why not?" he finally said. His tone was amused and overly patient, like he was dealing with an overexcited child.

"First," I said. "My terms. Remove your clutches from around Mike's heart and forget about him. He doesn't exist to you anymore."

"And what will I get from this? Other than a witch I can no longer control?"

"Oh, you'll still have your control." I took a steadying breath. "Release Mike, and I'll give you what it is you're wanting."

"Which is?"

"Witches willingly on your side. Myself, to be exact. I'll join your cause. Live on your mountain. Guard you, help you, whatever. Just let Mike go."

"And what guarantee will I have that you won't turn on me once I've given you what you want?"

He had a good point. "I would give you my word. Swear my services to you or something. There's a binding spell..."

"And yet, by keeping my...what did you call it?...*clutches* around your boyfriend's heart, I can have all of that with a lot less effort and a much stronger guarantee. Having his life on the line is also a much more effective way to keep you in line." He paused, pretending to think it over as his eyes traveled up and down my body and a look of disgust passed over his face. "I think I'll pass."

My heart dropped into my stomach and tears that I refused to shed filled my eyes. Of course, I should be used to it by now. I've never been anyone special. Not in my relationships. Not in the coven. I'm used as an extra spurt of magic when needed. I'm not someone anyone would fight for.

But I...I would fight for Mike. Because he was my friend. And I would do whatever it took to free him from the mess I'd created by making myself available to this mother fucker. All because I wanted a chance to flex my powers and get a little recognition.

The dagger burned against the skin of my lower back. But it wasn't ready. Fighting down my panic, I desperately tried to think of something he wouldn't be able to refuse. "Alice," I told him. "I'll give you Alice."

The djinn's eyes shot to my face. "Alice," he deadpanned. "My niece."

"Yes," I said, my voice gaining strength again. "I'll bring her to you."

He was still. So still I took a breath to beat back a wave of nervousness. "By what means?"

"By whatever means I have to use." I expected the surge of guilt that came as soon as the words left my mouth. What I didn't expect was the sense of loss that rose up within me now that the offer was on the table. We'd never really been friends, Alice and I, and honestly, I'd never liked her. She'd always been so sweet. So innocent. A brown noser. The exact opposite of myself. She'd always been around at family events and coven meetings and that, but she was never really a big part of my life.

But serving her up to the djinn...it wasn't sitting well with me.

However, I was running out of options. And maybe it would buy me enough time to figure something else out. But first I had to convince him this was the way to go. "It's what you came here for to begin with, right? To recruit your family? Well, I can help you with that. You've lost Alex, he'll never leave Kenya, but Alice...his sister...her I can get. But only if you release Mike from all of this and agree that he's off limits. He has no powers. No magic. He's of no use to you." I took a breath. "Agree to my terms and I'll bring you your niece."

"You would risk the wrath of your coven. Trade your cousin's life for your friend's."

In the coming darkness, I couldn't read him. Had no clue what he was thinking. "Yes. For you, I would do that."

He looked down at the sacred ground between us. I thought maybe he was smirking, but I couldn't really tell. "And what about yourself, Angel? What do you want out of this for yourself?"

"I want to be free of you," I told him without hesitation.

Tilting his head back, he studied the sky again.

He was playing with me. I could feel it. He wasn't going to go for my deal. Anger suddenly swept through me and I took a step toward him, sucking air in through my teeth as the dagger wiggled with the movement, searing my skin. "I'll bring you Alice! It's what you wanted! So, set me free!"

"And what of her brother, Alex?"

Immediately, I shook my head. "That's impossible. There's no way I could control him. And he's mated. Death itself couldn't keep him from her now."

He was silent for a long time as he studied me. I shifted my weight from one foot to the other, digging into the earth. "Does family mean nothing to you, witch?"

The air around me thickened and thinned, swirls of power brushing my cheeks and hands, but I didn't dare take my eyes off of the djinn. "I've never really had much of a family," I told him honestly. "Not close, anyway."

"I had a brother," he told me. "We were very close when we were younger. And then he betrayed me over a woman. A witch." He paused, lost in the past. "I never forgave him."

Yes, Alex had filled all of us in on the history. I felt like he was waiting for me to say something. "I'm sorry."

He toed the dirt with his foot. "Are you, though? Do you truly understand what it feels like to put your love, your *trust*, into someone, only to have them throw it in your face?"

Actually, I did. "Yes, I do." Adrenaline rushed through my veins. He was fucking playing with me. The air became so full of malice I started to breathe through my mouth in an effort to get more oxygen.

"And yet, you're doing this exact thing to my darling Alice? How do you think that will make her feel?"

He was fucking crazy. He was never going to consider my deal. "I'm just...trying...to show you...that I'm loyal..."

"Bullshit!"

He was suddenly right in front of me, his hand around my throat. I coughed and gagged as he lifted me with one arm until only the tips of my toes scraped the ground. I tried to pull his hand away, but he was too strong, his magic too powerful.

"You're standing here in the middle of an empty cemetery sacrificing your family to save your own pathetic skin," he ground out. "And that of your friend. A HUMAN! I should kill him, right now."

"NO!" Tears filled my eyes and ran down my face. I could barely draw air. "Please!"

But he only smiled.

Without releasing me, he lifted his other hand. From the corner of my eye, I saw him begin to clench his fist.

<u>Noooo!</u> Panic ripped through me and I reached behind me with one hand and pulled the dagger from the waistband of my pants. Magic sang through the blade, making it vibrate, and I tightened my grip on the handle so I didn't drop it. Bringing it in toward me, I sliced downward, right across his arm. I tried to cut his fist right off, but the blade wasn't powerful enough yet and I was weak from lack of air. However, it was enough to catch him off guard.

"AHHHH!"

I was suddenly free. The hand around my throat gone as he clapped it down over the deep cut in his arm. I fell to my knees and crawled backward, the dagger gripped tight in my fist as I tried to put some distance between us before I got up. But I couldn't get my feet under me.

The djinn speared me with eyes that now glowed, and I felt his magic curl around me as I fell backward, my head smashing into a tombstone. Scrambling around it, I kept my eyes on him as I used it for leverage to get to my feet.

"That stupid move is going to cost you, witch. Give me the dagger."

I glanced down at his arm, but he still had his hand over the wound so I couldn't see how much damage I'd actually inflicted. Throwing my free hand into the air, I sent a blast of magic straight at him. It was fight or flight mode time, and I was fighting. I wasn't going to let this fucking bastard take me out while I groveled at his feet.

My magic slammed into an invisible wall, reverberating through my teeth and bones. With a quick jerk of his head, the djinn sent me flying through the graveyard. I stopped when I hit another large tomb, my back smashing into the corner of the structure. I fell face first onto the ground, my spine screaming and the back of my head throbbing.

But I still had the damned dagger.

Slowly, painfully, I got to my feet, grateful I could still walk and that nothing seemed to be seriously damaged. Throwing up a shield of magic around myself, I ran back to him, dagger lifted to strike. I had to finish this. Or I had to die trying.

The djinn watched me coming, his face lit with amusement and perhaps a sliver of respect.

He waited until I was close before he made his move. One second he was there, and the next he was gone. Unable to stop my momentum, I ran into a smaller tombstone and toppled right over it, head over heels, landing on the back of my right shoulder and flopping over onto my back.

I laid there for a second, catching my breath. I'd come dangerously close to stabbing myself just now, and I needed a moment to be grateful I was still alive.

As I got to my feet once again, I choked back a sob. It was impossible. The only chance I had was this dagger in my hand, and I hadn't had enough time to finish the spell that would give it the power to kill a djinn. My magic wasn't strong enough. *I* wasn't strong enough.

I wasn't going to leave this cemetery tonight.

8

JAMAL

I searched The Quarter, but there was no sign of the redhead or anything that would give me any hint of where she might be. The weather was better tonight, and tourists crowded the small streets decked out in their best, or most ridiculous, holiday attire. Women lifted their shirts to show off red and green tassels with bells covering their nipples--among other imaginative body decorations--and the people on the balconies threw down Santa and Rudolph beads mixed in with the normal Mardi Gras colors of purple, green, gold, and red.

The humans paid me little mind as I made my way through the throngs of people, and I had no interest in hanging out to see what kind of show was offered. I'd seen it all before, and tits were just that. Tits. Some were big, some were small, some were more my taste than others, but after living here for so long and seeing the same thing night after night, it got kinda old. Even for a hot-blooded male. Unless seeing those tits was going to lead to other things, I wasn't interested.

"Where would I go if I were a witch who didn't want anyone to find me?" I mumbled out loud. I'd reached the end of Bourbon Street, and seriously considered turning around and marching my ass straight into The Purple Fang to make more productive use of my time. I'd already scoped out the entire area from I-10 to the waterfront with nothing to show for it, and I was seriously done playing bloodhound. But then, with a loud sigh, I crossed Canal Street and started walking toward the Garden District.

I hated coming to this part of the city, even if it was allowed now. As soon as I got within a block of the witch's hood, I could feel tendrils of magic reaching for me. Curling around me. Making its way beneath my clothes and slithering along my bare skin. I tried to just keep walking and ignore it, but the sensation made me grind my teeth together.

The witches would know I was here now. Although with any luck, they'd be too busy looking for Leeloo to fuck with me. I was beginning to wish I'd brought my car. But parking was more of a hassle than it was worth when I could run faster and not even work up a sweat. However, it did make me feel safer being here when I was surrounded by a frame of plastic and metal.

I had no idea which direction I should go or where she would be, but I thought her house would be a good place to start. Maybe she just wanted some alone time and wasn't answering her phone or the door. Pulling out my cell, I texted Lizzy and got the address. Five minutes later, I knocked on the door to her apartment, but it wasn't Leeloo who opened it.

Cocking my head and crossing my arms over my chest as I fought the sudden, inexplicable need to hit him just for being here, I stared at Mike, Lizzy's assistant. He was wrapped in some kind of ratty blanket and looked like he hadn't slept or eaten for days.

"Is she dead? She's dead, isn't she?" he asked as soon as he saw me.

"Who?"

"Angel." His features twisted as he fought back the tears in his eyes. "Who the fuck else would I be talking about, man?"

Something akin to rage made my fists clench under my arms. My gums tingled as my fangs slid down, aching to sink into his throat. I had no idea what I was so pissed about, but everything in me was protesting the fact that this human male was at her place, had apparently been here for a while, and was pretty damn fucking comfortable there. "Do you know where she is?"

Mike's eyes lifted to my face and he took a quick step back, out of arm range, as he eyed me nervously. "Sort of."

I lifted one eyebrow in question and waited.

"She wouldn't tell me exactly, but it has something to do with...the djinn."

My blood ran cold, and for a moment, I couldn't even respond to that. "The djinn? The one that took Kenya?"

"And Alex. Yeah." He pulled the blanket closer around himself, as if all that soft fluff would somehow protect him from the big, bad monsters in the world.

"Why would she be messing with the djinn?"

His expression set into stubborn lines, and for a minute, I thought he wasn't gonna tell me. If I could get inside the apartment, I'd already have him up against the wall by the throat. But one, I hadn't been invited in, and unless his name was on the lease too--a thought that made me grind my teeth together--Leeloo had to be here to do it. And two, from the way the creepy crawlies were prickling my skin, she had some kind of ward set up to protect this place.

Either he read the look on my face or just happened to have a good sense of self-preservation, because he took another step back. "Have you ever been here before?"

He knew I couldn't get in without an invitation, but I wasn't about to give that away. "Where exactly is she, Mike?"

He shook his head. "I don't know."

"Jesus fucking Christ." I scrubbed my face with my hands as I tried to get a grip on my patience. Dropping my arms back to my sides, I stared at him. "Did she say she was going to meet the djinn? Those words exactly?"

Again, he shook his head. "She wouldn't tell me anything about where she was going or what she was doing."

"Then how do you know she's fucking with the djinn?"

"I just do."

"And you didn't think to maybe, oh, I don't know, try to fucking stop her?"

"She's a witch, Jamal."

"And?"

"And you know damn well I wouldn't be able to do a damn thing about it if she has her mind made up to do something."

As I waited for him to say more, I dug into his mind. Not too far, I didn't want to see anything I didn't want to see--if you know what I mean, just enough to see if he was telling the truth.

He was.

"Satisfied?"

I focused my vision in on his face to find him giving me a disgusted look. "Yeah," I told him. "I am." Surprisingly, I felt no shame for breaking my number one rule of staying out of the heads of others.

I stared at him a while, hoping an explanation would appear from his mouth. But after a minute, I gave it up. This was getting me nowhere. I turned to leave.

"Jamal."

Swallowing my impatience, I stopped and gave him my attention.

"She's been gone for days. I'm scared..." He broke off, unable to finish what he was obviously thinking. "Please. Find her."

Crossing my arms again, I leaned against the doorframe. "Why aren't you out looking for her if you're so damned concerned?"

His mouth twisted in frustration. "That's a long story, but I also promised her I'd stay here."

I could see I wasn't going to get anything else out of him, so after running my eyes over him in a way that left him with no doubts at all about what I thought about him cowering in her apartment while she was possibly in trouble, I shoved off the doorframe and stalked back down the hall, not stopping until I was out in the fresh air.

Taking a few deep breaths, I tamped down my anger and refocused. Looked like Leeloo didn't have anyone else coming to her rescue. So that left me.

All right, then.

My phone buzzed. Pulling it out of my pocket, I glanced at the screen. It was Lizzy.

>*Any luck?*

>*Not yet*, I told her. *Just checked her place to make sure she wasn't here. Will let you know if I find anything.*

>**Sigh** Ok. Thanks. I'll keep calling around.*

Shoving my cell back into my pocket, I started toward the home of the high priestess. She wasn't there, but maybe Leeloo was hiding out or something. But I'd only gone about a half a block when I caught a faint scent on the cold breeze. One that made my throat burn with thirst.

Blood.

And not just any blood. Leeloo's blood. I would recognize her scent anywhere. "Son of a bitch."

Closing my eyes, I let my instincts take over. Let the hunter inside of me come to the surface. My nerve endings tingled as I concentrated on the night around me. I heard the faint sounds of someone playing a jazz horn and smelled the spicy, meaty scent of gumbo and rice. Humidity from the Mississippi clung to my skin. And the buzz of insects vibrated in my ears.

I separated the different scents and sounds, concentrating on the distinct smell of my witch. With a low growl deep in my throat, I followed it through the Garden District to one of the many cemeteries. At first, I saw nothing but tombs. But then I heard a low, warbled cry, and my head snapped around to find my witch hovering in the air near a large marble chamber. Her back arched to the point of snapping her spine. Her mouth open on a now silent scream.

Every cell in my body burned with rage, and my eyes snapped to the male below her, his arms held high as he laughed at her pain.

Baring my fangs, I jumped the fence and rushed headlong into the fight.

9

ANGEL

Shit. Shit. Shit.

I hung suspended in the air, fighting like hell to keep this bastard from snapping my spine like a twig. Agonizing pain shot from the middle of my back like bolts of lightning, traveling up into my chest and shooting down my legs and arms.

I fucked up. I fucked up big time.

As I struggled to breathe against the pain, a ringing started in my ears, blocking out his words. His mocking laughter. Black dots spotted my vision and I fought to stay conscious.

My magic wavered, and my back arched another inch. I tried to scream as something popped and practically choked on my own spit, the dagger falling from my fingers to clatter on the rocks below me, but I had no breath. Praying it was only a joint in my spine and not a disc that had made that noise, I gritted my teeth and gathered the remains of my strength, sending out a shot of magic.

The djinn laughed when he felt it, staggering back a small step before pushing forward again, and I remained hovering a good seven feet up from the ground.

I was going to die. He was going to snap me in half and leave me here to rot with the rest of my ancestors.

A deep, feral growl echoed through the tombs, ominous and inhuman. Even in the excruciating state I was in, little hairs all over my body stood on end, sensitive to each vibration of whatever the hell it was I was hearing. I turned my head right as the djinn did, my vision blurred with tears, as something as violent as the night and transparent as the mist rushed toward us. It hit the djinn dead center, knocking him backward.

As soon as his hold was broken, I fell to the ground, landing hard on my sore back, but thankfully just missing a marble cross sticking out of the ground. Carefully, I curled into a ball, relieved when I found I could, as horrible sounds ripped from the djinn's throat. I didn't know what was killing him, and I didn't care, as long as he was out of my life. Out of all of our lives.

I should've known it wouldn't be that fucking easy.

As the fight seemed to take a turn, I found the dagger on the ground and picked it up, then staggered to my feet right as the djinn threw off his attacker. He flew through the air, landing less than six feet away from me. I peered down at him. He was wearing black jeans and a black, short-sleeved shirt. His dark skin marred only by the streaks of djnn blood dripping down his chin. "Jamal?"

Eyes black as night flew to my face and latched onto me. When he saw me there--bent over with tears streaming down my face--he flashed white fangs and flipped onto his feet, again facing the djinn. With measured steps, he stalked closer, fangs bared and hands curled into claws.

He was terrifying.

He was beautiful.

He was every evil thing's nightmare.

One hand on the mossy tombstone beside me to use as a crutch, I took a couple of hesitant steps back. Other than a slight twinge, my back didn't give me any problems. Slowly, keeping my eyes on my unlikely savior as he circled the djinn, I used my arm to push my upper body up until I was standing straight. Nothing seemed to be seriously hurt, and I breathed a sigh of relief.

But a moment later, my heart was racing as Jamal charged the djinn.

Even with one side of his throat torn open and blood covering his white button-down shirt, the djinn stood tall and strong, waiting for Jamal to get closer before he struck. I saw it too late. "Jamal! Don't!"

Before he could get a hold of him, Jamal once again went flying through the air. Only higher this time, flipping head over feet as he flew over my head, straight toward a large tomb surrounded by an iron fence. I watched in horror as he came down directly on top of the pointed finials topping each post with the force of something much heavier than him. Two of the spikes tore through him, spearing him there like a fish. He hung over the fence, his back arched, much as I had just moments ago, a groan escaping him as his hands floundered around the spikes that had gone right through him.

A scream began somewhere down in my gut, fighting its way up through the horror that froze my lungs. I smashed both hands over my mouth before it could escape, the dagger still gripped in my hand.

"This conversation isn't finished, witch."

The words came from directly behind me. I spun around, eyes wide and my hands still over my mouth, but we were alone in the graveyard.

The dagger fell to the ground as I dropped my arms to my sides and rushed over to Jamal, but I stopped just short of touching him. "Jamal?" His name was little more than a throaty whisper.

His only response was a sound somewhere between a groan and a growl, full of pain and...regret.

"I'll get you off of there," I swore. He would survive if I could just get him off of this damned fence. Right?

Right?

"He will," I told myself. "He's a goddamn fucking vampire. Nothing kills him."

"Leeloo..."

My eyes jerked up to his face. He didn't look so good. "Yeah?"

"Stop talking..." he took a shallow breath, "and get me down."

"Right." Taking a deep breath, I closed my eyes and felt for my magic. I was exhausted after fighting for my own life against the djinn, but it was still there. Just a smidgeon, but it was enough. Throwing a quick prayer to the gods, I drew it up from my core, feeling it tingle through my blood, flowing through my body, stretching toward the tips of my fingers and all the way down to my toes. I forced it outward until I found Jamal, and heard him curse as it touched him, surrounding his body. Carefully, I put some force into it as I tried to lift him off the spikes.

He cried out as I lifted him. I don't know how far I got before my muscles began to shake and I began to sweat with effort.

"Angel!"

My name was little more than a gasp and I opened my eyes. Jamal was still on the spikes, but the tips had disappeared somewhere inside of him. His head was raised, and his hands were gripped tight around the fence to either side of him as he tried to help me.

Holding him steady with my magic, I crouched down and got underneath him as close to the fence as I could, balancing him on my shoulder. Moisture seeped through layers of my clothes to wet my skin, and I knew from the coppery smell it was his blood. He was losing a lot of it. I needed to get him off this thing so he could heal himself.

Using both physical strength and magic, I pushed up, my legs shaking with effort. Somehow, I managed to lift him up and off the spikes. With a grunt and a curse, he leaned forward, toppling over me and onto the ground.

As soon as he was off the fence, I fell forward and landed on my stomach on the ground, my entire body trembling with the effort it had taken me.

Jamal lay above my head, curled in on himself with his back up against the tomb across the path. A dark puddle formed beneath him, growing faster than the ground could absorb it.

I crawled closer to him, ignoring the moisture that seeped into the knees of my jeans, and peered at his face in the darkness. His eyes were closed and his dark skin ashen. "Jamal?"

His only response was a barely audible groan.

"What can I do?" I asked him.

He didn't answer.

Was it that he couldn't? Or he just didn't want to talk to me after he'd nearly gotten himself killed rushing to my rescue. "What the hell are you even doing here anyway? I didn't ask for your help, vampire."

There was no response.

Carefully, I reached toward him, checking his wrist for a pulse. I wasn't sure I felt anything, so I went for his neck. His nostrils flared as my hand got close to his face, and too late I remembered the gash in my palm made by the dagger when the djinn was throwing me around before suspending me in the air like a rag doll. The cut still burned from the magic the blade was infused with, and was still bleeding freely, though not nearly as bad as the vampire.

A low growl rumbled deep in his chest, and his eyes shot open. I stared into the dark orbs as they searched blindly for the food source he smelled, looking for the male I'd talked to before, but he wasn't there. There was no sign of anything human in those black depths. Only pain. Only hunger.

Ever so slowly, I started to inch my arm away from his mouth, afraid to move too quickly. Although we witches had lived with the vampires for many years now, I'd never seen one quite like this. I always thought they were more like the old Dracula movies when it came to seducing their prey to feed, not like this creature who was more animal than human.

His upper lip pulled back from his teeth, and long, white fangs lengthened before my eyes. An eerie hiss raised the little hairs all over my body and I froze. "Jamal?" I tried to talk to him, hoping maybe the sound of my voice would pull him out of this state he was in. "Hey! Jamal. Snap out of it, dude. I don't have the energy for this right now."

It was the truth. I was exhausted.

I started to set my arm down to rest on my thigh, and like a snake spotting a warm-blooded mouse, his eyes grabbed onto the movement and zeroed in on my hand.

Blood was still pooling around us, leaking from the holes in his torso. Not as fast as before, but enough to show he still wasn't healing properly.

Fuck. Maybe I should just feed him. It would help him, right? To get some fresh blood in his system? Give him some strength to heal himself? "I'm probably going to regret this," I whispered more to myself than him. "But..." I paused, took a breath, and thrust my bloody palm toward his mouth. "Here you go."

I expected him to pounce on what I offered, much like the serpent I'd compared him to earlier, but he didn't. Instead, he became very still. One hand came up and he wrapped it around my wrist. His tongue flicked toward the open wound. Testing. Tasting. Another growl sounded deep in his throat, and then his fangs sank into the flesh of my hand right below my thumb. I jumped with a wince when he did it, even though I was expecting it. It didn't hurt, not much anyway. His teeth were super sharp and slid through the skin and muscle with ease. Not like human teeth. I watched with something akin to fascination as he held me to his mouth.

And then he started to drink...

10

ANGEL

My breath caught in my chest as each pull he made went straight from my hand to my womb, sharp jolts of desire that had me squeezing my thighs together. I moaned in disappointment when he released me and I felt his tongue on my skin, closing the wounds he'd made. But he wasn't finished yet.

Faster than I could track, he yanked my arm closer to his mouth and latched onto my wrist. Deeper this time. He moved, curling his body closer to mine, wrapping around me like a constrictor. And it was only then that I began to feel afraid.

He was wounded and not in his right mind. What if he didn't stop on time? I knew he could; otherwise, they'd be dumping bodies out the back door of their club every night after they'd fed. But that didn't happen. The ladies walked out of there on their own two feet, usually with a goofy smile on their faces. I'd witnessed it myself.

Lizzy. I should call her. She would know what to do. I couldn't call Aunt Judy, she was too far away to help. Besides, she'd kick me out of the coven once she found out what I'd done and why I was here. And even though Lizzy and I didn't know each other very well, I had a bone deep feeling that I could trust her to keep her mouth shut. She was new to the area and to the coven, and therefore her loyalty didn't run as deep.

I hoped.

Plus, she was mated to Killian. A vampire. And Jamal was one of his. She wouldn't do anything to put him in danger.

Fishing my cell from my front pocket with my free hand, I awkwardly turned it on, waiting for the little apple to go away, then navigated the touch screen with my left hand, punching in the code since my phone was programmed to unlock with the fingerprint from my right thumb. Lizzy's number was in my favorites, as were the rest of the witches in my coven. She answered on the second ring.

"Angel? Where the hell are you? Everyone's been worried. And where is Mike?"

It didn't surprise me that she skipped right to Mike. He was the only one she really cared about besides these damn vampires. I closed my eyes. I shouldn't be like that. One of those "damn vampires" just saved my life. And was now draining the blood from my body. "I need your help," I told her. "With Jamal."

There was a pause. "Jamal? Did he find you? What happened?"

"I can't explain over the phone." A wave of dizziness hit me. "Do you think you could come here? He's hurt. I'm giving him some blood, but I don't know what else to do."

This time there was no hesitation. "Of course. Where are you?"

I gave her the location of the cemetery and hung up, grateful I'd had the forethought to keep my cell in the tight pocket of my jeans where I wouldn't lose it. And that's where I returned it. I didn't bother to turn it off this time to save the battery. I needed to go home and regroup before I gave spelling this dagger another try.

Another wave of dizziness hit me. I rode it out, and when the world straightened again, I looked down at Jamal. His color was better, and it looked like his wounds were finally trying to heal. I couldn't really see for sure though without lifting his shirt. But he was wrapped around my right hip and drinking from my right wrist, so it was kind of hard to reach him.

I tried to pull my wrist away from his mouth, but he growled at me, his dark eyes flashing to my face and his hold on my arm becoming even tighter. A warning.

A jolt of panic shot through me. But then I took a deep breath and calmed my ass down. He was looking better. Surely, he would stop when I asked him to. "Jamal, you need to stop. I'm getting lightheaded and I'm cold. You can't take anymore."

He ignored me.

"Jamal!" I yelled in his face. "Let me go!"

When he continued to feed without showing any signs of letting up, I knew I had to do something. I'd be dead by the time Lizzy showed up if I let him keep going. "I'm sorry," I told him.

Closing my eyes, I pulled on my magic, hoping I'd had enough time to replenish it. I didn't need much, just enough to knock him off of me. I gathered it into the center of my body, then sent it flying, concentrating on my right arm and hand where he was holding me.

It hit him like a zap of electricity, and he released me, jumping to his feet so fast it was like he was laying there on the ground one second and the next I was staring at his hard thighs and the large bulge in between them. All I'd have to do was rise up onto my knees again and he'd be right at mouth level...

Jesus. What the hell was I thinking? Once again, I scrambled to my feet. My eyes snapped up to his face. Slowly, he cocked his head to the side as those dark eyes drilled into mine. His fangs were still bared, my blood on his lips. His posture was strong, alert, in full-on hunting mode, different from his normal relaxed pose. He seemed bigger, stronger, and way more dangerous as he tracked every tiny move I made.

Swaying on my feet, I threw up my hands in front of me and his eyes zoned in immediately on my still-bleeding wrist.

"Whoa there, dude. You need to back the fuck up and get a grip on yourself."

His answer was little more than a deep rumble that seemed to come from the center of his chest.

"Jamal." I tried again to talk to him. "You have to stop drinking from me now. I want to help you, I do, but I can't give you any more blood. We'll have to find you a new donor." That seemed to piss him off, if the lifted upper lip and irritated hiss he gave me were any indication.

Looks like this vampire had gotten a taste of witch and didn't want to go back to a bland human.

I opened my mouth to try to convince him they weren't so bad when he was suddenly on me, those long fangs going for my throat. Catching myself just in time, I sent out another blast of magic, the tips of his teeth scratching my skin just before it punched him back, his boots sliding in the dirt as he fought me. He stopped about ten feet away and tried to lunge at me again, but I was ready this time and held him where he was, my magic around me like a forcefield.

When he realized he couldn't get to me, he began to pace like a caged animal. Back and forth. Back and forth. His eyes never left me, flicking from my face to my bloody wrist and back again, over and over, just waiting for me to weaken. A constant low growl vibrated the air around us, irritating my magical shield. But I knew if he got to me again, I wouldn't survive. All I could do was hold him off until Lizzy got here and could help me.

Long minutes passed by as I waited. By the time I heard the screech of brakes and Lizzy calling my name, I was shaking, my entire body trembling with fatigue. With one look, she rushed up to Jamal and stepped in front of him. "Jamal! You need to back away."

"Get away from him, Lizzy."

At Killian's tone, she stepped away. Although, honestly, she probably didn't need to. Jamal hadn't given any indication he'd noticed her there, even though she was standing right in front of him. His entire focus had been on me, as it had been for what seemed like the last hour, but probably wasn't that long.

Fuck. She'd brought Killian with her. Anxiety rose within me. I didn't want to tell him what was going on. What I'd done. He'd kill me for sure for bringing the djinn here, for putting Kenya in danger. She was his favorite, everyone knew that.

Killian stepped up next to me and glanced at me sideways. "Release him."

"I can't." My voice was little more than a rasp.

"You can. I won't let him hurt you."

"Are you sure about that?"

He made an affirmative noise, his eyes on his friend.

"Okaaaay..." Gods, I was gonna regret this. "Ready, set..." I dropped my hands and drew in my magic, stumbling back into Lizzy's arms. "Thanks," I told her when she kept me from falling on my ass.

"I've got you," she said.

The instant the shield was gone, Jamal's eyes lit up from within and he lunged. I closed my eyes and threw up my arms to try to protect myself as best I could, but he never touched me.

I cracked open my eyes to see Killian had stepped directly in his path. Jamal didn't stop in time and his large body wrapped around him before he pushed off and focused on this new threat that was keeping me from him. Killian stood tall and strong as the tombs surrounding us. He hadn't even flinched.

"Do you want to hurt her, Jamal?" He pushed him off as Jamal rushed him again. "Stop! Look at her. She's hurt. Do you want to hurt her more?"

Jamal's dark eyes skipped over to me. I'd fallen to the ground the moment I saw Killian had him under control, despite Lizzy trying to hold me upright. She was beside me, checking my hand and wrist where I'd ripped him off of me, leaving deep wounds. She pressed on them with her bare hands, trying to stop the bleeding.

"She's MINE." His voice was like something you'd hear in a horror movie, but the words were discernible enough.

I froze when I heard it. As did Lizzy. Then I felt her hand clasp my arm and she squeezed. "Don't move," she whispered.

"You don't need to tell me," I hissed back. Holy shit. I was being claimed by a vampire. He'd tasted me. And now he wanted more. Can't say I blamed the guy. I'm sure I was quite a treat to a blood-starved vamp, but he'd have to get in line behind Mike if he wanted things to go any further than that.

I almost giggled out loud. My head was foggy and the cemetery was starting to spin around me. Without conscious thought, I tried to lift my arms to Jamal. Safety. He was safety.

Lizzy pushed them down into my lap, again applying pressure to the tears on my right hand.

"I know she is, my friend," Killian told him. "I know she is. But you're going to hurt her if you don't get a grip on yourself."

I saw it the moment Jamal's body language changed. His stare shifted from me to Killian, who gave him a knowing nod. His eyes, black as night, narrowed in disbelief. "What the fuck is happening?" Jamal asked him, a note of panic replacing the possessive growl.

"He's hurt," I told them. "The spikes on the fence went right through his stomach."

But when Killian went to grab his shirt, Jamal knocked his hand away. "I'm fine." The words were gritted out between his clenched teeth. "What. Is. Happening. To. Me."

There was a long pause. "I think you know," Killian finally told him.

Jamal shook his head. Fast and hard. "No." He started to pace again. Not like earlier. This was more of a "I can't believe this is happening and walking back and forth will either help me process it or make it not be true" kind of nervous energy. A moment later he stopped. Taking a step forward, he got up in Killian's face. "I will not be chained to THAT WITCH." The words were spit out in disgust, right in Killian's face, but he held his ground. "Isn't it enough that I'm chained to you?"

"What is he talking about?" I whispered, fighting to keep my eyes open. Lizzy just squeezed my arm again.

But I really didn't need to ask.

I knew.

11

JAMAL

I couldn't stop myself from staring at Leeloo.

I knew that wasn't her name. But it suited her. Because this goddamn witch was no angel. If anything, she was a demon straight from hell sent here to torment me. I had to remember that.

Maybe that's all that this was. Some kind of spell she'd cast on me when she offered me her blood. Because there was no fucking way my instincts were right. No way this voice in my head that was screaming one word over and over again wasn't some trick of her making. No way every damn cell in my body sang for one other person's blood and one other only till death do us part.

No *fucking* way she was my...*mate*. I could barely think the word, let alone say it. That shit wasn't even real. And I didn't care that Killian and Kenya would say otherwise. They're both in love, not *fated* to be with those people. Nah. I shook my head as I stared at her, this woman I barely even knew. This was bullshit.

Yet, even as I tried to deny it, my body hardened from the sight of her standing there. It prepared to hunt. To feed. And to fuck. She was disheveled, dirty, blood soaking her clothes--both mine and her own. Nothing like the picture-perfect image she usually made whenever she walked into a room. And even from this distance, I could smell her. Her blood mostly, sweet and spicy and the best fucking thing I'd ever tasted. But other things, too. Her skin. Her hair. Even the musk between her legs.

I bit off the groan that nearly escaped when I thought of burying my face between her pale thighs. Tasting her there, too. My mouth began to water.

"Jamal?"

As the hunger for her blood refocused into a completely different kind of hunger, I forced myself to look at Killian. It was the most difficult thing I'd ever done. "What?" I bit out.

"Are you all right, then?"

My maker's Irish accent was both familiar and hated. "Yeah," I lied. "I'm good."

"How is your stomach?"

"It's fine."

"May I see?"

"No," I told him. "You may not." With one last look at the redhead on the ground in Lizzy's arms, I spun on my heel and walked away. I'd found the bitch for them, now they could deal with her.

"Jamal! Wait!"

I heard Lizzy calling me, and then I heard Killian telling her to let me go.

Enough. I was done. I should've taken off the other night instead of hanging around and sticking my nose into witch business. Nothing came from that shit but getting on the wrong side of a djinn. I was damn lucky one of those spikes hadn't gone through my heart.

But as I ran back to the house in The Quarter, my blood sang through my veins, reminding me of the mouth-watering outcome of the injuries I'd sustained. Gritting my teeth, I refused to acknowledge the differences in Angel's blood and how it affected me. It was just because she was a witch and therefore had magic inside of her. That was all. That was why every single cell in my body was buzzing with electricity. Why I could hear every nuance of the wind, the swish of each blade of grass, every tiny footstep of a rodent at a house blocks away, see colors in the night sky I'd never noticed before, and pick out nuances in the air I'd never smelled before. And why the scent of the humans in the homes I passed made me want to vomit.

It was why I could still *feel* her, no matter how far I ran.

The extremity of the physical lust? Yeah, that I couldn't explain, except for the fact that I've always been attracted to her and maybe it was just all of that pent up tension suddenly being released.

When I got home, I saw lights on in the main house. I stopped in the middle of the courtyard, staring through the windows like a creeper as the vampires who had become my family joked and laughed and went about their nightly routine, unaware they were being watched.

One side of my mouth twitched as Brogan planted a big kiss on Dae, laughing as Dae swatted him away and cussed him out in Korean.

I would miss this.

I watched them for hours, retreating into the shadows when Killian and Lizzy got home. Until everyone started wandering off to their rooms for the day and the lights started to go out one by one. The sun would be up soon, and the automatic blinds would come down. I'd take the day to get my things together, and then I was out of here. Away from this witch and her clingy magic.

It briefly occurred to me that I might just be in denial. What if my stubborn ass took off out of here only to find myself starving for my mate's blood? If this shit was true, I'd be dead within a matter of months. Maybe weeks.

But then I had to wonder, did it really matter? I thought about that for a minute. Really thought about it. Was that what I wanted? Honestly, sometimes the thought was tempting. But...FUCK. I just wanted my own life. My own choices. I grew up in chains, and I felt like no matter what I did, I couldn't escape them, although they changed over time. Sometimes they were shorter. Sometimes longer. Sometimes the links were easier to break than others, but they were always fucking there. Maybe they weren't always made of iron, but they were there, nonetheless.

And a blood bond between a vampire and his or her mate? That was the strongest fucking chain of all. More unbreakable than the one that bound me to Killian.

It made me feel weak. And I fucking despised that feeling.

"Jamal?"

The moment I heard her voice, my entire body shot to attention. A second later, her scent washed over me like a waterfall. My nostrils flared, her sweet and spicy blood gaining my attention first and foremost, and my gums burned as my fangs descended. A deep growl intensified within my chest as I turned to look at her, and I couldn't quite contain it as I asked, "What are you doing here, Leeloo?"

She was pale, and still looked a little shaky, but her eyebrows rose at the sound, and she held her ground. I was glad to see she hadn't lost her sass. "I just wanted to make sure you were okay. And tell you thank you." She twisted to the side, pointing toward the gate, which I just noticed was open. "Killian said I could come in, and to tell you to sleep well and call if you need anything."

It came to my attention that my body wasn't upright anymore. Instead, it was swaying toward her, sheer stubbornness the only thing keeping my boots rooted to the ground. I forcibly straightened, denying myself the pleasure of her nearness. "There's no need for that."

She didn't say anything for a long moment. "So, are you? Okay?"

I assumed she was talking about my injuries. Honestly, I hadn't bothered to check. But I didn't have any intestines hanging out and I didn't hurt, so I guess everything had healed up fine. "I'm good."

She glanced up at the sky where the first streaks of dawn were starting to appear. "Should we go inside?"

I shook my head. "Nah. There's nothing else for us to discuss."

"But there is," she protested. "And I want to explain--"

"You don't have to explain anything to me, Leeloo." Although her hazel eyes shot fire, her hands twisted together nervously in front of her, and my eyes dropped down to her blood-stained sleeve. I pointed at it with my chin. "How's your arm?"

She gave a nervous laugh. "Uh...I don't really know. I haven't checked it."

"Don't you think maybe you should do that?"

"Yeah," she nodded, "I will. I just wanted to talk to you first."

Taking a deep breath, I ignored the thirst that burned the back of my throat and rubbed my forehead with one hand, trying to ease the sharp pain that had suddenly sprung up there. It didn't help, so I stuck my hands in my pockets and tried taking some more deep breaths. "Look, you don't have to explain anything to me. You got yourself into some shit. But he's gone. Just...don't wander around alone anymore."

She smiled, but it didn't quite reach her eyes. "It's not quite that simple."

"Why not?"

The smirk fell from her face. "We both know why, Jamal."

Gods, I loved the way her lips wrapped around my name. I wondered if they'd look as good wrapped around my cock. Blood rushed to my groin, every muscle hardening along with my sex. Clenching my fists at my sides, I tried and failed to calm the hell down as the lies came out of my mouth. "No. I don't think we do."

Her gaze dropped from my face to my throat, taking in the strained tendons before going lower to my clenched fists and the bulge in my jeans. I gritted my teeth together, hiding my fangs from her sharp eyes. When she finally spoke, her voice was low and throaty, "Are you hungry?"

Fuck, yes. I was fucking starving. And not just for blood, but for flesh. Specifically, hers. Even covered in jeans and a hoodie, I could still make out the shape of her body, and my palms burned to feel that soft, pale skin covering all of those curves. "No," I ground out.

After a moment's hesitation, she took a step towards me. "I think you're lying."

"Why are you fucking doing this?" I burst out. "You got a death wish? Is that what this is?" My skin prickled in warning of the coming sunrise, and yet I couldn't get my feet to move from this spot and take me inside. Hell, maybe she came here to murder me. To hold me captive in her witch's spell as the sun rose and she could watch me burn to ash. After all, I was the only witness to what had actually happened back there in the cemetery. She could've told them anything after I'd left.

"I don't want to hurt you," she said softly. "Just the opposite."

I stared at her hard. "What?" I asked. "Ya gonna save me, Angel?"

"I don't want to see you die because you're being too damn stubborn to admit what happened between us."

"Nothing happened," I told her. "Except you throwing your magic all at me."

She laughed. Like threw back her head and laughed out loud. I glanced up at the sky. I didn't have time for this shit. Lifting my upper lip, I bared my fangs at her and forced my feet to move. This secret rendezvous she'd trapped me into was gonna have to come to an end. My skin was gonna start sizzling any second now. I only made it a few steps before my body took on a will of its own, my steps slowing as I glanced back over my shoulder at her. The pull to run back there and scoop her up into my arms to bring with me was so strong, I nearly acted on it without thinking.

Still chuckling here and there, she watched me try to fight my way into the house.

"Let me go," I said through my teeth.

"I'm not making you stay," she responded.

I hissed in pain as the sun peeked up over the horizon and smoke rose from my exposed skin. Fucking witch was about to burn me alive. I opened my mouth to call for help, but then I shut it again.

Let her do it. Maybe then I would be free.

12

ANGEL

Stupid damn vampire would rather stand there in the sun and burn to death than admit he and I were now a "thing." And I meant that term loosely. I mean, come on. Was I really that bad?

I fought back a sudden rush of tears, blinking them away. What the hell did I care if he liked me or not?

The truth of it was I didn't care. Not in the way you'd think. But the fact that it was so abhorrent to him to even consider the fact that fate had chosen me as his mate...something sad and angry twisted inside of me. It wasn't like I was thrilled with this whole arrangement, either. But at least I wasn't such an ass that I'd just let him run off and starve himself to death.

Because as much as he tried to deny it, I could see the way he looked at me. The way he...*hungered* for me, even now.

I wasn't sure how to handle all of this, to be honest. I mean, I barely knew the guy. But on the other hand, the gods do what they do. And as far as I knew, there was no way to break the blood bond once it happened. And come on, the guy just saved my life. The least I could do was return the favor.

So I walked toward him, watching him closely. When he hissed at me, warning me he was about to strike, goosebumps chased each other across my skin, but I only hesitated for a brief second before I rushed him and pushed him up against the doors of the building he'd been heading toward when I got there. Reaching around his lean waist, I ignored the deep growl that vibrated his entire chest cavity, opened the sliding door, and shoved him inside. Then I slammed it closed behind us, sending up a quick thank you to the gods that it hadn't been locked. That would've been awkward. Other than stiffening up when I threw myself against him, he'd made no move to stop me or push me away.

But as soon as we were inside, I stepped back and put some space between us, using the doors behind me to rest against. Then I waited to see what he would do, ready to defend myself if need be. His dark eyes tracked every subtle movement I made, his nostrils flaring wide as he scented me, but otherwise he was completely still.

As I watched and waited, I wondered how old Jamal was. That would tell me a lot. Older vampires had a lot more self-control than newer ones, but of course it was impossible to tell just by looking at him. I didn't know if that self-control applied to mated vampires or not, but it wouldn't hurt to know. "When were you born?" I asked quietly.

He stood eerily still, like he was carved from stone, the way only a vampire could. Every muscle in his body coiled tight. Watching. Waiting. His entire being focused on me. It was unsettling. A nervous shiver slid down my spine and I mentally calculated the time it would take me to get back out the door and into the sunlight that was beginning to warm my back through the glass.

"You won't make it." His voice was calm enough, but I didn't miss the underlying tone of danger.

"I might," I argued. "I've had a chance to rest a bit. I think I have it in me to zap you again if I needed to."

His chin raised in a sudden motion of defiance, but then he smirked as his body once again became animated, turned, and walked further into the house, taking off his leather jacket and tossing it on a navy upholstered chair. "Are you asking when I was born? Or when Killian made me into a walking dead thing?"

"The second one."

He glanced up at me a moment, his eyes searching my face, and then sat down on the edge of the matching couch. Resting his elbows on his knees, he looked up at me. He appeared calmer now that he was in the shadows and not so close to me, away from the direct sunlight I stood in. "I'm old enough," was all he said. "I'm not going to attack you, if that's what you're asking."

"Are you sure about that?"

"Positive," he deadpanned. "I was injured earlier. Lost a lot of blood. The only reason I wouldn't be able to control myself now is if you were...more to me than any other human. Either by magic or other means. So, if you do have some sort of spell on me, it'll be no one's fault but your own if I drain you dry."

This guy was unreal. "You're still hung up on that, huh?"

His only response was a grunt.

I laughed, but there was no humor in it, only disbelief. "So, you seriously think I just spent three days in a cemetery tomb making some kind of love potion I could ingest, just a-*hoping* you would show up and drink from me, so I could make some guy I barely know think he was my new vampire husband? Why the hell would I do that? What would I get out of it except a severe case of anemia?" I stared at him, waiting for him to realize how stupid that sounded and laugh with me about it.

He didn't.

"What *were* you doing there?" he asked. "And how the hell did you wind up in a fight with a djinn?"

My smile faltered. New vampire husband or not, what would he do if or when he found out it was me who'd told the djinn about Alex and Alice? Who'd put the female vampire--his friend--in mortal danger? I had no idea how he would react, but I would bet money it wouldn't be good. So telling him how I'd ended up there was out. However, I could give him a partial truth. "I was there working on a spell to kill him. But he found me before it was completed."

His eyes, which had wandered down around my hips, flew back to my face. "You were going to take on a djinn alone? Are you fucking crazy?"

"Maybe," I replied. "But somebody has to do it."

"And why do you feel that someone should be you?"

Ah, my vampire saw too much. But I just shrugged, playing it off. "Why not me? I'm one of the more powerful witches in our coven." Wandering away from the door, I kept one eye on him as I made my way slowly across the room to the chair that sat catty-corner to the couch. He watched me closely. I could see he was still tense, but he made no move toward me. Actually, he was back to playing statue.

"How did he know?" he suddenly asked.

"Know what?"

"That you were there?"

I paused for the briefest of moments. "I don't know."

His dark eyes narrowed. Just the tiniest of movements. "And now you're lying to me."

"I'm not," I lied.

He cocked his head but said nothing. However, his dark eyes drilled through mine as I held his stare. The muscles around my eyes twitched, and I suddenly felt like I was no longer alone. I mean, of course I wasn't alone. I was sitting here in the same room with him. But in my head. I wasn't alone in my head.

Too late I realized what was happening and I threw up my shields. Aunt Judy had taught us all how to do it, but this was actually the first time I'd had to. "Get out of my head, Jamal."

His eyes widened slightly, the expression on his face hard to decipher, then his jaw set into a stubborn line. "Stop lying to me, Leeloo."

I looked away and took a deep breath. He couldn't have seen much, or he wouldn't still be sitting there so calmly. When I turned back to him, I schooled my expression into one of boredom. "Look, that's not why I came here."

"Why *did* you come here?"

That was a good question. I stood up from the couch. "Know what? You're right. I shouldn't have bothered." I strode to the patio doors, the hairs on the back of my neck rising as he watched me leave. But he didn't try to stop me.

I stepped out into the morning sunshine and turned to close the doors behind me. Jamal had risen from the couch and now stood just out of the circle of light. I jumped when I saw him. I hadn't even heard him move. Slowly, never taking my eyes from him, I slid the door closed.

It wasn't until I was out of the courtyard and walking down the sidewalk toward the nearest streetcar line that I remembered I was still covered in his blood. And mine. And yet, the vampire had controlled himself.

Maybe I wasn't as irresistible as I thought.

13

JAMAL

Disgusted with myself, I used my mind to lock the patio doors and keep that fucking redhead out. Covering my face with both hands, I pressed my fingertips against my closed eyelids, wishing I could undo what I'd just done.

I'd broken my number one rule without even thinking about it. Just because I couldn't stand the thought that she was hiding something from me. And it was all for nothing anyway. All I'd been able to pull from her mind was an overwhelming sense of fear and some distorted images before she blocked me.

What the hell was it about that female that made me forget any morals I somehow managed to cling to?

You know what it is.

I flashed my fangs at the empty room. Nah. Fuck that.

Dropping my arms back down to my sides, I strode down the short hallway to the bedroom and attached bath at the end. I needed to get the hell out of that room and away from the scent of her. Try to get some sleep. I was working at The Fang tonight. And with any luck, I'd find a meal with big tits and juicy veins to take my mind off of that damn witch.

"What's up, man? What's happening? What's going on?"

Elias greeted me from behind the bar as I walked into The Purple Fang just after sunset. I lifted my chin in greeting as I pulled up a stool. We still had about thirty minutes until we opened the doors, and I wasn't on until the last show, but I couldn't stand being in my own head anymore. I needed other people around. Something else to focus on besides a certain red-headed witch. Before he could ask me anything about the night before, because I could fucking guarantee things were said after Killian and Lizzy got home, I said, "That woman is hanging around again."

He looked up from the paper he was writing a list on and raised one eyebrow. "Which one?"

"Dark hair. Red lipstick. Always dressed in red, too. With a black, leather jacket."

Elias shrugged and went back to his list. "She has a thing for guys who wear tacky Hawaiian shirts."

"Brogan?"

He scratched the back of his neck. "She's only here on the nights he's working."

"So, he has a stalker."

"Maybe." Elias didn't sound concerned, and neither was I. We were used to it. And if it got too annoying, all we had to do was have one of us--usually Dae Jung because he had no morals--give them the suggestion that they weren't that into us. Human women found us irresistible. Not because we were all that. Not really. I mean, we were all decent looking guys as far as that went, but it was the vampire thing that really got them. We were predators, and nature had made it easy for us to attract our prey.

I was kind of glad, though. I don't know how I'd feel if we had to truly hunt for our meals. Take down a human like a lion takes down a gazelle. It was hard enough to hang on to our humanity as it was. Although there were some like me who did hunt like that, who got off on it, I wasn't one of them.

"So I hear you got yourself a girlfriend."

I glanced up to find Elias's black eyes laughing at me. "You heard wrong."

He ignored my protest. "I'm just glad it's you and not me, man. Ain't no woman gonna have *me* at her beck and call, messing up my room with all of her stuff."

"You gonna make her have her own room?"

"Hey," he stopped what he was doing and stared at me with a perfectly serious expression. "There's nothing wrong with having a little order in your life. I know the rest of you don't appreciate it..." Setting the list he'd made near the register, he grabbed a towel and started wiping down the spotless bar. "Well, maybe Killian and Lizzy..."

I interrupted him, having no desire to listen to his spiel on cleanliness. "I don't have a woman."

Something in my voice must've finally gotten through to him, for he stopped what he was doing, and the smirk fell from his face as he stared at me across the bar. "That's not what I heard," he told me, but he wasn't busting my ass anymore. He was dead serious.

"What did you hear?"

"That you saved that hot little redhead from a fight with a djinn and got yourself impaled for your efforts."

I hated to even ask. "Anything else?"

He sighed, set down the towel, and leaned his elbows on the bar, large fingers rubbing the back of the opposite hand. "I heard you drank from her. That she offered it to help you heal. And that when Killian and Lizzy got there you were pacing in front of her like some sort of starved beast. Liz said you looked like Killian had the first time he drank from her."

I let out a nervous laugh. "Nah, man. They're exaggerating." I touched the center of my chest. "I was there when that shit happened. It was nothing like that. I'd just lost a lot of blood. That's all."

Elias stared at me until it was fucking uncomfortable, and I suddenly knew how he always managed to get the underage drinkers into confessing without dipping one toe into their heads.

"What," I said.

He dropped his chin, breaking eye contact. But just for a second as he got his thoughts together. "Look," he told me. "I talk a lot of shit. I know this. But Jamal, if you've found your mate--"

"Leeloo is NOT my mate."

"If you've found your mate," he continued, a little louder this time, "then it is what it is, man. Fighting it will get you nowhere."

I couldn't believe what I was hearing. "Don't tell me you believe in that shit."

He straightened, pulled out his phone, and checked the time. "I know what I see in front of my own damn eyes. First Killian. And now Kenya. Something is in the air, and I have the feeling we're all gonna be fucked eventually. And not in a good way. You just happen to be next." He lifted his chin toward the door. "Wanna get that? Time to open up."

I slid off my stool. "Who's up first?"

"Dae-Jung. Then Brogan."

I nodded. Dae was a great opening act. He always got the audience all wound up for the rest of us. That guy's hips got the cash flowing better than alcohol. Or maybe it was the massive tattoo on his back the ladies liked. Either way, it worked.

While the other guys warmed up the stage for me, I sat in the back office, thinking about what Elias had said. I was so deep in my thoughts I didn't hear Kenya when she came in to do the books.

"Hey," she said softly. I could hear the concern in her voice even over the music.

"Hey," I said. "How are you?" Although I don't know why I even asked. The female shone from the inside out like she had her own personal sun in there.

"I'm good." She smiled. "How are you?"

That was a loaded question. "I'm good." I stood up, hoping to make a quick exit.

"Jamal, wait."

Fuckin' A...almost made it. Turning back toward my friend, I lifted one eyebrow in question. "Sup?"

"'Sup?' That's all you have to say?"

I shrugged, playing it cool. "Is there something else you want to talk about?"

She gave me a disbelieving look for a second, then sat down behind the desk and gave a pointed look at the chair I'd just vacated. With a deep sigh, I retook my seat. Leaning back, I spread my hands wide. "What?"

"You were almost killed last night, that's what."

I waved away her concern. "Nah. It wasn't that bad."

"That's not what I heard." Her dark eyes appeared larger than normal through the lenses of her black-rimmed glasses. Or maybe it was just my own guilt that made me squirm on my chair.

"Well, you heard wrong."

"I heard you got into a fight with a djinn trying to save a certain witch, but you lost, and that you got impaled in the process." She gave me the same look my momma used to give me when she knew I was full of shit. "Is that not what happened?"

I released the breath I'd been holding and gave it up. I couldn't lie to Kenya. I never could. "Yeah, that's what happened."

Satisfied, she logged into the computer, her attention on the screen as she asked, "Why the hell are you going off and doing something stupid like that?"

My eyes on the floor, I said, "I don't know. Lizzy asked me to help find her, and you know I can't say no to her." When I looked up, she was watching me. "What?"

"You know, being mated isn't so bad--"

I launched myself out of my chair. "Ah, Jesus fucking Christ! Not you, too. That's not what happened!"

"Jamal." Now she even had the "mom tone" in her voice. "There's no sense in fighting it."

"I'm not fighting anything!" I yelled, throwing my arms in the air. Then I stopped. Took a breath. "It didn't happen," I repeated, emphasizing my words by slicing my hand through the air. "I was hurt. I was bleeding out. She offered to feed me, and I took it. Maybe I was a little overzealous. I hadn't fed in a while, I was trying to heal, and I had to stop drinking before I was ready. That's all."

"Have you fed again since then?"

"No. I plan to do that tonight."

"Have you *wanted* to feed again?"

An odd sensation crept up my spine. "Why would I? You know I don't need blood that often. Honestly, I don't even need it tonight. I'm just going to do it to prove my point."

One eyebrow went up, but she pressed her lips together and gave her head a little shake.

"What are you getting at, Kenya?"

She scrolled through whatever she was looking at on the screen, all casual-like. "I'm just saying that the first time I drank from Alex, I knew. I just knew. And now even just the thought of drinking from someone else makes me gag."

"Yeah, well, I don't know nothin' like that." *Liar.*

Her hand stilled on the mouse and her eyes swung my way, her expression drawn in with concern. "What are you so afraid of, Jamal? Other than knowing that if something happened to them, you'd follow right along shortly after?"

I pointed at her. "That. That right there. I spent my entire human life in chains, passed from one owner to the other. And when I finally managed to escape this godforsaken life, I woke up again only to find out I had a new owner. This time a vampire who was so lonely for a friend, and still is, that he denied me my peace." I slapped my chest. "My CHOICE. It was my choice to live or die, and Killian took that from me. And I don't even have the balls to destroy the monster he made me into..." My words faded away, along with my indignation. "I know he thinks he did the right thing by me. That he 'saved' me." I made air quotes with my fingers.

"But you don't see it that way. I know that. But being mated...it isn't the same thing, Jamal."

My lips twisted into an ugly smile as the fight suddenly drained out of me. "Isn't it? All I'm doing is trading in one set of chains for another. She's not my mate, Kenya. She fucking owns me now. I can't survive without her. Can't drink from anyone else. Can't fuck anyone else. She holds all the power over my life." I sank into the chair again, letting the truth sink in. "*Fuck* me."

"Jamal..." Kenya came out from behind the desk to squat down in front of me, her hands on my knees. "From one brown-skinned person to another, I get it. I totally do."

I knew she was trying to commiserate, but she *didn't* get it. Not really. Kenya hadn't been born a slave. She'd never had to spend her days working in fields until every muscle in your body screamed until you thought you'd never be able to stand straight again, your hands were blistered and raw, and your throat was like sandpaper, only to get beat for not picking fast enough and have to do it all over again the next day. Only this time bloody and bruised. She never lived off one meal of mush a day. Was never torn from her family.

Never saw her sister raped over and over again by the white man who'd bought her like a piece of cattle. "I was gonna leave," I confessed. "I was finally going to be free."

She leaned back to look up at me. "What? When?"

"Right before all this happened," I told her. "I was packing a bag. I was fucking out of here." I knew my face was covered with all of the pain and regret that was tearing through me by the way she was looking at me. "I was about to be free, Kenya. For the first time in my fucking life. I was going to be *free...*" I choked on the words as a sob wracked my body.

14

TALIN

Seattle, WA

The raven stared at me with one beady, black eye. I tried to ignore her, but it was kind of hard, even though she was on the other side of the living room perched on her owner's shoulder.

Golden topaz eyes turned my way, and the warlock whose shoulder she rested on raised his hand to ask the woman speaking to him to pause a moment. He was dressed all in black. The only color coming from those strange glowing eyes.

"I'm not her owner," he told me. "I'm her friend. She's here because she chooses to be."

I glanced at my aunt, the person he had been speaking to. But she gave me no indication by word or expression how I should respond to his comment. As a matter of fact, her face was carefully blank. I couldn't really blame her. We were all semi-terrified in his presence. The power emanating from him while he spoke calmly to the high priestess of our coven was intense. I couldn't even imagine what he was like when he was angry.

And now we knew he could read our minds. What the hell kind of warlock was he?

"I'm sorry," I told him. "I meant no disrespect to either of you. And I'm sorry for interrupting your conversation," I included Aunt Judy here.

"It's all right," he told me. "Talin, was it?"

I nodded and he continued, "Many people make the same mistake."

The female vampire beside him with the dark hair and green eyes much like my own laid a hand on his shoulder in a possessive gesture. I smiled at her, trying to ease the tension, and after a moment, she smiled back, an apologetic look in her eyes.

The bird was still staring at me, and I raised my pierced eyebrow at her in question. She made a sound like a deep gargle into the warlock's ear.

"She wants to know if she can play with your eyebrow ring," he told me.

"Uh..." I had no idea how to respond to that, either the bird's question or the fact that he could understand what she was saying.

"Cruthú," the female vampire--Shea, I think her name was--scolded the bird. "You don't have to play with every shiny thing you see." She turned her green eyes to me. "She loves to play with my earrings." Then she shrugged. "I guess what they say is true."

"Um," I eyed the large bird. "I don't know that I want that beak so close to my eye."

The warlock, Jesse, laughed. "I was only telling you what she wanted, so you wouldn't be startled if she suddenly decided to visit you. I didn't want you to think she was trying to peck out your eye." He scratched the bird's feather-covered neck. "She likes you. Probably because you remind her of Shea."

"I seriously can't keep her away from me," Shea said, but although she tried to sound annoyed, a smile teased her lips and affection shone from her eyes when she looked at the raven on her mate's shoulder.

Everyone's attention was on me, and I fussed with my white, long-sleeved T-shirt and the dark gray vest I wore with my jeans, making sure it covered my chest so as not to draw attention to it, even as I tried to look like I wasn't being all fidgety. I found vests were a great addition to my normal ensembles. They provided additional layers and coverage without being too hot in the summer and not too cold in the winter. They're kind of my signature look now.

But I needn't have worried. After a few amused looks, everyone went back to paying attention to the conversation that was back in session between Aunt Judy and Jesse. My entire coven, except for Angel, was in Seattle visiting the coven here, led by Keira Moss. Even Alex had left his new mate, hoping he and Alice could talk to the warlock who had saved their lives and had blood ties to them.

Their vampire mates were in attendance also. It made for a packed apartment, but the view over the city from the ceiling to floor windows behind me was breathtaking.

As the warlock went back to what he'd been saying, I glanced around at my Seattle witch cousins. Keira stood beside Judy, her arms crossed over her chest and her dark head tilted as she listened. Her mate, Luukas sat in the chair beside her, but one hand rested on the back of her thigh, rubbing his thumb against the soft material of her yoga pants. He was the master vampire here, and his power also swirled throughout the room. But there was something else, something I couldn't quite put my finger on, that was strange about him. Whatever it was, it frightened me. Like maybe he wasn't quite stable. But that was impossible, right? How would he have power over so many vampires if he wasn't right in the head?

Shaking off the thought, I let my eyes wander over the others. Luukas's brother--Nikulas--the blond with the Hollywood good looks and easy smile, and his strawberry-blonde mate--Emma--who had horrors I couldn't even imagine deep in her hazel eyes. The vampire in the hoodie--Aiden--who looked like some sort of middle-Eastern prince with his dark looks and bright gray, laughing eyes. His mate, Grace, had the most gorgeous, long auburn hair and pale skin. She also called him "dude" a lot, which he pretended to hate but I think he secretly loved. As I watched, he made a face and reached behind him, adjusting the hood of his hoodie. A small face peeked over his shoulder, little black nose twitching, before it disappeared again inside the bed it had made for itself in the vampire's hood. I wanted to take a closer look to see if it was what I thought it was but didn't know if Aiden or the thing in his hood would appreciate me interrupting its nap.

Then there was Christian, the tall, dark, and silent type who exuded a sexual energy I could feel all the way over here. His mate, Ryan, was stunning with her hair like the sunset, white skin, and sapphire blue eyes. But she was just as quiet as he was, and never left his side. There was something haunting about her. Something I couldn't quite put my finger on.

But the scariest one? At least where the vampires were concerned? Yeah, that was definitely Dante. He stood as close to the front door as he could get and still be considered as one of the group. The guy was huge and muscular, his dark skin tattooed in black ink all the way down his left side from what I could tell. He stood behind the couch directly behind Laney, his mate, with his fists clenched at his sides. And every few seconds his eyes would drop down to the top of her chestnut brown head, then he'd glance over his shoulder toward the door. His energy gave me the impression that he was like a stick of dynamite, ready to explode at any moment. And I wasn't sure if that explosion would protect us or hurt us, although the rest of the vampires and witches didn't pay him any mind, so I tried not to let him worry me. However, so far I'd managed to keep myself as far away from him as I possibly could.

"...much do you want me to say in front of the others?"

My ears perked up. Aunt Judy glanced at Alice, Alex, and myself. But he wasn't talking to her. His question was directed toward Luukas.

The master vampire didn't hesitate with his answer. "I have complete trust in my vampires and their mates. And I'd think you would also need to have that same trust in your coven. The djinn needs to be stopped, and that's not going to happen if we're keeping secrets from each other."

Aunt Judy agreed. "Go ahead," she told the warlock. "Say what you have to say."

His eerie eyes went to Shea, then to Ryan. She gave him a nod.

I looked at the pretty redhead again, wondering what her connection with him was.

Jesse reached up and ran his hand over the raven's feathers. I'd already picked up that it was what he did when he needed something to steady him. There must be quite a history between the man and the bird that they were that close. "I know who helped the djinn the night we rescued Alex and Kenya."

Aunt Judy showed absolutely nothing of what she was feeling on her face. "Who was it?"

"One of your witches."

Her eyes shot to Alice, then me, before going back to the warlock. I'm sure we looked just as shocked as she was. "That's not possible."

"I'm sorry to have to tell you this. But it's something you need to know so you can protect yourselves."

"And how do you know this?" my aunt asked him.

The raven made a deep, raspy call, fluffing her feathers as though she was offended by the human's question. Jesse reached up and ran his hand over her feathers to calm her. "I was told by things who see far more than I do."

"Things?" Aunt Judy asked him. "What sort of 'things'?"

I had a perfect view of the warlock from where I stood, so I saw the way his jaw tightened and how his mate placed a hand on his back, petting him much the way he had the raven.

"He's telling the truth." Ryan spoke up, and I wasn't the only one who turned a shocked face toward her. The only one who didn't seem surprised was Christian, her mate. "My brother and I can speak to...spirits, I guess you would call them. They watch over us and tell us things that we wouldn't know otherwise."

Aunt Judy glanced over at Luukas, the master vampire, for confirmation. "I've never found anything he's warned me about to be false." Though his words rang true to my ears, there was something in his eyes when he looked at the warlock that told me these two were not friends.

My aunt looked at the witch beside Luukas, and when she nodded in confirmation, she turned back to the warlock. "All right. Let's say I believe you. Who is it?"

"I don't know her name. But they told me she has bright red hair and hazel green eyes. And she is not here," he finished.

Holy shit.

He was talking about Angel.

15

JAMAL

I stood just off stage, rolling my head on my shoulders and trying to shake off this damn funk I'd gotten myself into. The music changed as it morphed into my stuff, and I pushed everything out of my head except the stage and the heavy beat that was now throbbing through my veins stronger than my own pulse.

Dancing was the only thing that ever lightened my soul. It was just me and the music. And nothing could touch me.

But as soon as I jogged out onto the stage, high five-ing Brogan as he came off, my senses came alive. And it wasn't the music that caused this particular reaction.

She was here.

I felt it deep in my bones, even before I glanced into the audience and spotted her bright red hair sitting at the bar with Elias. She was wearing ripped up jeans, high-heeled boots, and a soft-looking, creamy sweater with studs on the shoulders. Red lipstick made her full lips glisten.

She sat on that stool like she had every fucking right to be there. Like she belonged here, surrounded by vampires. And it pissed me right the hell off. There was no doubt I was the reason she decided to catch the show. As soon as I walked out onto the stage, her gaze zeroed in on me and locked on.

But I had no time to confront her about shit. It was my turn to put on a show.

Determined to ignore her, I started to freestyle, working my way across the stage and grinning wickedly at the human women who crowded around the stage, waving cash at me. And I was still fully clothed in black pants hung low on my hips and a plain, white T-shirt.

Losing myself in Eminem's beat, I danced.

I'd hoped the witch would leave when she'd seen enough to know I wasn't going to pay her any mind, but I should've known better. I was down to a black g-string with ones and fives poking out all over when I finally deigned to give her an ounce of attention again. Defiance written all over my face, as if to prove she didn't own me--whether to her or to myself, I didn't know--I grabbed the best-looking woman I could reach and pulled her up onto the stage with me.

It didn't escape my notice that the woman had red hair, however, it was nothing like Leeloo's. Her lips weren't the color of blood, and she was dressed all in yellow, a color I'd never seen on Angel. She looked like a summer picnic, one any man with eyes would like to lounge around in all day. Quite a different vibe from the perfectly put together witch with her narrowed cat eyes watching me from the bar. I didn't want to spend a lazy day inside of her, I wanted to rip her expensive clothes off her delectable body and fuck her hard against a wall. Wanted to leave marks on her pale skin so she wouldn't be able to look at herself in a mirror without remembering I was there. I knew just by looking at her that witch was no sunny day, she was a summer storm. Hot and wet and full of electricity that would shock my system until I craved nothing but her.

I left my guest squealing in excitement with her friends as I walked off stage and grabbed a wooden chair. Setting it behind her, I took her hand and indicated for her to sit down, kissing the back of her knuckles. Her flowery scent hit me hard, too cloying, and I tried not to wrinkle my nose in disgust as I flashed my "fake" fangs at her. Her eyes widened, but she smiled big and glanced down at her friends as I started to dance around her and tried not to think about the sweet spice of the woman at the bar.

Going around behind her, I grabbed the seat and picked her up, chair and all, spinning her around before putting her back down. Jumping up, my feet on the side rungs, I gyrated in her face, her hands on my thighs, trying to pull me closer. I waved my finger at her playfully and shook my head, then backflipped away before dancing up close again. Leaning down, I grabbed the chair behind her head and tilted it back, my face in her cleavage...

The chair was suddenly yanked from my hands and the woman fell backward, landing on the floor and sliding between my spread legs and halfway across the stage.

What the fuck?

The ladies in the crowd "ooh'd" and "ahh'd" like I'd meant to do that shit, and I played along even as my mind went through all of the different ways that could've happened. I kept coming up with the same answer: there was only one natural way, and there was *no* way I'd dropped her. These little chair tricks took barely any effort at all.

Jogging over to her, I straightened the chair to seat her upright again and grinned, playing it off, my hand on the back of her head to check for a lump as I leaned down and asked if she was okay. She assured me she was fine, her hand drifting to my bare chest. It took effort on my part not to push it away, which was weird. I was used to being touched, and it normally didn't bother me at all unless they got too insistent about it.

Suddenly, her hand abruptly flew back, like it was attached to a string and something was pulling her away from me. At the same time, a few of the lights above the stage busted, raining glass down onto our heads. Everyone who'd been crowding around the stage screamed and backed away, falling over chairs and tables as they went.

What the actual fuck?

My eyes flew to the bar where Angel was now on her feet, eyes wide, like she couldn't believe what she was seeing. But there was no surprise on her face. Only a cloud of guilt.

Her gaze clashed with mine over the heads of the women teetering toward the exit with drinks in hand, then she turned and gathered her coat and bag from the stool beside her and joined the throng, pushing her way through the panicked women in an effort to escape.

Elias stood behind the bar with a bottle in one hand watching it all go down. I signaled to him and pointed at Angel. With a nod, he jumped the bar and easily closed the distance between them. Luckily, everyone was too worried about getting the hell out of the bar and paid no attention at all to the bartender who covered twenty feet in a quarter of a second. Reaching around a young blond, he caught Angel by the arm and hauled her out of the chaos, pulling her back against his chest and locking her there by wrapping both big arms around her.

By the time I arrived beside them, the air was thick with magic, slithering over my bare skin, and Elias was trembling with the effort to hang onto her as she zapped him, but there was a wide grin on his face. Little did she know, Elias liked pain almost as much as he liked an orderly bar.

"What did you do?" I demanded over the music.

"Tell him to let me go," she ordered.

I gave Elias a nod. He gave her a warning squeeze around her waist, grunting when she zapped him one last time, then dropped his arms and released her. I tried and failed to stop the possessive sound that erupted from my chest when he didn't release her immediately. But Elias wasn't offended, he just grinned and wandered back behind the bar.

I half expected her to try to take off again, but she only glanced at the back of the group trying to push their way through the exit door and made a face. When I looked to see what was causing that look, I saw my stage partner, arms linked with her girlfriend, talking animatedly as they both kept glancing back over their shoulders at me and then the stage. Like they expected the exploding lights to follow them or some such shit.

Humans were fucking ridiculous sometimes.

"Wanna come with me?" I asked her.

She hesitated, looking down at the floor, then shrugged.

"Don't touch that," I told Elias, indicating the broken glass. "Leeloo here will clean it up when I'm done with her."

Her expression hardened, but she lifted her chin defiantly and didn't say a word.

"Come on." Taking her cold hand, I pulled her behind me, heading toward the office.

Kenya stood at the entrance to the hallway, watching the commotion. Her brown eyes danced with amusement as I approached, hauling a reluctant witch behind me.

"Can I use the office?" I asked her. I would take Angel to the back room, but I wanted privacy. Or as much as could be had with two vampires and their supersonic hearing lurking around.

"Sure," she said. "I was just waiting for Elias to cash out the bar." She leaned to the side to look around me and smiled. "Hey, Angel."

"Hey, Kenya." She didn't sound near as happy to be there as Kenya was to see her.

I pulled her past my grinning friend and into the office, closing the door behind us, but not bothering to lock it. It would be a moot point anyway if anyone really wanted to get in. Witch or vampire. As soon as we were inside, I released her hand and put mine low on my bare hips. "You wanna tell me what the hell that was out there?"

"Magic," she answered without hesitation. Her eyes dropped to my chest, then my stomach, and lower for a brief second before they flew back up to my face. "Do you think you could put some clothes on maybe?"

"No," I told her when I got over my shock at her honest answer. I'd expected lies, excuses...something. Not a straight up honest answer. "Why did you do it?"

This time there was a brief pause. "I didn't like her touching you. And I didn't like you so close to her."

"You didn't..." The words faded away. Again, not what I was expecting. "That's what I do here. It's how we bring in money."

Crossing her arms over her chest as best she could with her coat still in one hand and her bag in the other despite Elias's manhandling, she rolled her eyes. "What do you need money for? Unless you guys are just really bad at investing." Those hazel green eyes travelled down the length of my torso again. Only this time when they dropped lower, they stayed there. The tip of her tongue wet her red bottom lip, making it glossy.

Jesus fuck.

I could feel myself, already half hard the moment I got within three feet of her, grow harder still under her heated stare. "Angel." I barked out her name. I was about to bust out of my G-string.

Her eyes, when they flew to mine, were more green than brown now.

"You need to stop looking at me like that," I gritted out.

"*I* told *you* to put some clothes on," she retorted.

"What are you even doing here?" I asked her, changing the subject, cuz this particular argument wasn't going to get us anywhere but equally naked.

Her chest rose and fell on a deep sigh, then she set her coat and designer bag on one of the chairs in front of the desk. When she turned to face me, she looked just as bewildered as I felt. "I don't really know," she said softly. "I just...I don't know. You were in my head."

I knew exactly what she was talking about. Though I wasn't about to be as straight up about it as she was being. "So you decided to come crash my show?"

"I decided to come watch your show," she corrected me. "The crashing part wasn't planned and surprised me as much as it did you." She pressed those blood red lips together and wouldn't look me in the face.

"Eyes up, Leeloo," I told her when I caught her eyeballing me again. If I had any sense of self-preservation, I'd do as she asked and put some clothes on. But some masochistic part of me was really liking the way she couldn't keep her eyes off of my near naked self.

She didn't do as I asked. "But I like looking at you," she said softly. "And isn't that the whole reason you do what you do? So women will look at you?"

"Other women, yes. You? No." It was a cruel thing to say. I knew that. And it almost had the desired effect I was hoping for. Almost, but not quite.

She went completely still for a long moment, a disbelieving smile fluttering around her lips and then dying. She narrowed her cat eyes and took a step toward me, green fire in her eyes.

"Stop," I told her.

Ignoring my order completely, she kept coming, slow and steady, until she stood so close the fullest parts of her breasts brushed my chest with every breath she took. In her heels, the top of her head came right about to my nose, but I still outweighed her by about eighty pounds of muscle. Not that it would help me if she decided to go all witchy on me. The A/C kicked on, the vent behind her blowing air our way and her scent overwhelmed me in a rush, the self-control I'd been hanging onto by a string flying out the window. My gums burned as my fangs punched down and I opened my mouth on a hiss.

A visible shudder swept over her at the sound and her eyes dropped to the razor-sharp points. I could hear her pulse pounding, fast and hard. Could hear the rush of her blood through her veins. The strong beat of her heart. I could smell her hair, the clean scent of her skin, the spicy sweetness of her blood, and the musk of her arousal. Feel her warm breath on my collarbone. "Leeloo..." There was a warning in my voice. A warning she chose not to heed.

"I can't stop thinking about you," she whispered. "About what it felt like when your fangs were deep in my wrist. How every time you pulled on my vein, I could feel it all the way to my womb. I'm aching right now, just thinking about it."

Her hand came up between us, ghostly white against my dark skin. Carefully, she placed it flat against my chest. I couldn't stop the moan of pleasure her touch conjured from deep within me. "What are you doing to me, witch?"

16

ANGEL

Gods, I didn't know. I had no idea what I was doing here or why I'd even come to this place. I just couldn't stop thinking about him. That night with the djinn kept playing over and over in my head, but still, I knew I should stay away. I didn't need Jamal asking any more questions. Or worse, just pulling them out of my head. I couldn't get too comfortable around him. Couldn't let down my guard.

But I wasn't lying when I told him I ached for him. It was true. I did. I didn't understand it, but it was there. Was this all a part of it? The whole mating thing? Ever since the night he'd taken my blood, I had an uncontrollable urge to give him more. Give him anything he wanted. My blood. My body. Anything except the reason I was in the graveyard to begin with. "Please," I whispered. I didn't know what I was begging for. His touch, maybe? His bite? "Please," I repeated.

Jamal stared down at me, more beast than man, his dark eyes nearly completely black. Gods, he was beautiful. All smooth, dark skin and powerful muscle. His hair was shaved close to his head, faded down to nearly nothing on the sides. His lips were full, but not too much. His nose straight, his jaw strong, and he had the cheekbones of a model.

But his good looks weren't the reason I was here tonight. No. There was something else pulling me to him. Something primordial. As old as time itself. My blood sang for him whether he was near me or not, even as my mind told me the smart thing to do would be to keep him as far away as possible. It was how I knew the truth of us, even if he tried to deny it. "Please," I begged him.

An animalistic growl rumbled through his chest, raising the little hairs on the back of my neck. I'd never been so aware of my physical body. I was a witch. Although I enjoyed dressing it up, my body was just a vessel for my metaphysical self. I was fire and air and magic, not this primitive creature who wanted nothing more than to writhe in the dirt with this male.

But right now, I would give up everything I was just to feel his hands on my skin and his teeth slice through my skin.

"Angel."

My name was a curse on his lips. I raised my other hand and placed it beside the first, pressing down until I could feel his heart pound hard against my palms. He smelled so good, and

I licked my lips, wishing I could taste his skin. His mouth. His cock.

Up until then, Jamal had stood eerily still. But suddenly, his hand was wrapped in my hair, yanking my head back as he ducked his head and took my mouth with his. His lips were soft and hard all at once, and he tasted like mint when his tongue swept into my mouth. He was rough and demanding, but not without finesse, and a surge of angry heat flashed through me when I thought about all of the other women he must've kissed just like this. But it was there and gone before I could focus on it as Jamal claimed my full attention. I winced when I felt his fang slice through my lip, but it was drowned out by his moan of pleasure.

"More," he growled against my lips. "I need more."

The fluttering in my stomach exploded outward and my legs went weak. I clutched at his shoulders in a desperate attempt not to fall to my knees, hoping I wouldn't drag him down with me.

But I needn't have worried. Jamal yanked me up against him with his free arm, holding me so tight against him I could feel the warmth of his skin and the hard length of him against my lower stomach. Tearing his mouth from mine, he kissed a trail of heat down my throat and past my collarbone, the light stubble on his jaw scraping my tender skin.

When he reached the neckline of my sweater, he drew back, his eyes questioning and my lipstick smeared across his mouth.

I stared up at him, the intensity in his eyes jarring me. I'd never had a guy look at me the way this vampire was at this very moment. Like a tornado could rip through the building and it wouldn't be enough to steal his focus from me. It was flattering and at the same time completely unnerving, and I wasn't sure exactly how to feel about it.

"Angel." His voice was pleading.

But what was it he wanted? My body or my blood? Or both? It didn't really matter. Right now, I would give him anything he needed, even if he drained me dry, just to escape my reality for a little while.

I opened my mouth to tell him I was his for the taking when suddenly he stiffened. His eyes flew to the door, and a moment later I was teetering on my high-heeled boots trying to lock my knees so I didn't fall and he was standing across the room.

But his eyes...those beautiful black eyes lit from within with some otherworldly light...never left my face.

My hand flew to my chest, and I forced myself to breathe. Just breathe.

A second later there was a knock behind me and Kenya called through the door, "Hey guys, sorry, but I need to get in there to finish things up so I can get home before the sun comes up."

"Just a sec," Jamal called out. His chest rose and fell with ragged breaths and his hands were clenched into fists at his sides. His black eyes tracked every tiny movement I made.

I told myself to move, to gather my things and get the hell out of there, but I couldn't get my feet--or any other part of me--to obey my orders. All I could do was stare back at Jamal. He appeared larger, his muscles harder, his erection thick and long and held against his stomach by his G-string. Even his face was changed. The bones sharper and his lips partly open, showing the tips of his fangs.

My heart began to pound out of my chest as he suddenly strode toward me. I watched him come, wondering what he was going to do, but at the last second, he swept past me and went to the door. I turned partially around and watched him crack it open, making sure to keep his bottom half behind the door. My eyes drifted down to his bare ass. Nothing but muscle there, too. Seriously, the dude could be the model for one of those Michelangelo statues...only with a much more impressive package.

"I need five more minutes," he told the vampire waiting on the other side.

"Jamal, come on..."

"Five minutes." He held up his hand, long fingers sprawled wide.

"Five minutes," she repeated. "Then I'm coming in."

He closed the door but didn't immediately turn around.

"Um, I can go." Walking over to the chair, I reached down to pick up my coat and bag. I'd stop by the bathroom on my way and fix my face before I walked out into the bar. I didn't know who all was still here besides Kenya, but I didn't want to take any chances of someone seeing me like this and word getting back to Judy. No, wait, what was I thinking? I could just magic myself up until I got home, not wasting any more time here than necessary.

Jamal grabbed my wrist just as my fingertips touched my coat, stopping me. "Stay a minute."

Straightening, I looked up at him, trying to ignore the fire still surging through my blood at his nearness. "Look, I shouldn't have come. I don't know what I'm even doing here."

His nostrils flared slightly, and I could tell he was scenting me. Although he didn't look quite as feral as he had a few moments ago, he was still a sight to see. If I wasn't a witch, if I was a normal human woman, I'd be terrified, instead of so turned on the slightest movement made my nipples rub against my bra and the ache between my legs grow so intense I felt like I was about to spontaneously orgasm if he didn't stop looking at me the way he was.

"Come back to my place with me."

I laughed. "All of a sudden you want me around?"

"I think we need to talk."

Surely, my expression reflected the level of disbelief I felt at that statement. And apparently, it did. Because a second later he dropped his eyes and rubbed the back of his neck before glancing up at me again. He sucked in his full bottom lip and seemed to consider things.

"Look, you were right. Okay?" he finally said, though he didn't sound happy about it. "And I think we need to talk about what's happening here."

Unexpected relief flooded through me, making me sway on my feet again. But it wasn't because I was all desperate for a boyfriend, I could have one of those whenever I wanted. I wasn't sure what it was, exactly, but the feeling was there. I reached out to take his hand, but he jumped back out of my reach so fast it was like he'd moved between one blink and the next. He closed his eyes tight for a second before focusing on me again. "You can't touch me right now."

I frowned. "Why not?"

Crossing his arms over his chest, he threw my own look of disbelief back at me, glanced down at his still-hard cock, and then back up at me.

Ah. I see. "Okay." I put both hands up in surrender. "I won't touch you."

But his voice had lowered a few octaves when he said, "So, you'll come home with me?"

I thought about it. Was I ready for this? But it didn't really matter if I was ready or not. This mating had happened. And now we needed to figure out how to live with it, because the last thing in the world I wanted was to see this beautiful male wink out of existence. I could be a bitch at times, but I wasn't completely heartless. And hey, I'd be totally down for some amazing vampire sex in the process. At least that was what I told myself. The real reason I was so gung ho about this teased the edges of my brain, but I pushed it away.

"Okay." Picking up my coat, I put it on and then grabbed my bag. Remembering I had a compact mirror, I pulled it out and checked the damage. Not as bad as I'd thought. I fixed my lipstick with a wave of my hand, Jamal watching me the entire time, closed the compact, and dropped them both back into my bag. "Let's go."

"Sure. Soon as you clean up the mess you made out there." He lifted his chin in the direction of the stage, then turned and walked away. "I'll get dressed and meet you out there." Leaving the door open, he left me alone in the office.

And after the view he'd just given me, I couldn't even be mad. Besides, it would take me all of two seconds.

17

JAMAL

I got Leeloo through the courtyard and back to my place without anyone seeing her. Or, at least I hope I did. I had enough to worry about right now without getting my balls busted by the guys.

Inside, I took her coat and laid it over the back of the chair. When I turned back toward her, I stilled, my heartbeat in my ears as I looked at her. This woman standing in my home for the second time, was a little surreal to me. Mostly because she was way out of my league. Her scent quickly filled the room as it had the last time she was here, and I clenched my jaw hard, holding my breath and trying to suppress the urge to let my fangs come out to play. "Would you like something to drink? I've got water or tea, both hot and cold."

She looked surprised. "I didn't think you drank anything but blood."

"Personally, I usually don't. I can, but I don't. But Lizzy comes over here sometimes. The tea and shit is for her."

"Oh." Something I couldn't quite read flitted across her pretty face. But it was there and gone before I could read it. "Um, some hot tea would be nice. Thanks. Whatever you've got."

"Sure thing." Grabbing a cup and a teabag from the cabinet, I ran hot water through the single cup coffee maker. "I don't have any cream or sugar or anything..."

"Black is fine."

The tension in the air racketed up when I took the cup to her, her fingers brushing mine as she took it from me. "Thank you," she said softly.

"You're welcome." I stayed where I was, caught in her cat-like stare.

"You wanted to talk?" The innocence of the question was betrayed by the husky quality of her voice and the earthy scent of her rising desire. My own need responded in kind, my dick hardening until it pressed painfully into the zipper of my jeans and my fangs busted through, no matter how hard I tried to stop them. Overwhelming thirst burned the back of my throat, and I took a few quick steps back.

Angel watched me closely the entire time, but though she cocked her head with a look of curiosity, she didn't comment on my sudden retreat.

When I thought I had myself under control, I took a deep breath. Yes. Better. "Do you wanna sit?" I gestured toward the couch.

"Yeah, thanks." She took her tea and sat down on the edge of the cushion on the far end, her hot tea cupped in her hands. They were trembling.

"I'm not gonna hurt you, Leeloo."

She laughed quietly. "Oh, I know."

I saw she hadn't completely lost her cockiness, and I was glad.

"It's just...this is a little awkward, ya know?"

"It doesn't have to be."

She eyed me over the teacup as she blew on the surface, saying just before she took a sip, "Still is, though."

"Yeah." I rubbed my palms together, trying to warm them up with some friction. I don't know why I always felt so damn cold lately.

"Jamal, please sit down. You're making me nervous."

"Sorry." I took a seat on the opposite end of the couch, as far from her as I could get.

She eyed the distance between us and the way my left side hugged the arm. "Am I that abhorrent?" she teased. But there was a flash of something else behind her smile. Pain. Something I knew well.

"No, not at all," I quickly tried to reassure her, but I don't know how convincing I was. I still tried, though, because the thought of causing her any kind of pain made me feel like someone had stabbed an icepick through my chest. "It's just...easier for me not to be too close to you."

"Easier how?"

But I didn't want to get into all that right now. "Look, I asked you here so we could talk about what's happened between us, and how..."—I took a breath, bracing myself—"...we're going to live with it." I clasped my hands together and looked down at the floor. I didn't want her to see the look on my face right now, because I'd think it would be kind of hard to miss the anger and disgust that was rising in me like a volcano. And the last thing I wanted was to explode all over my living room. I was attracted to her, yeah. Of course I was. And she smelled so *fucking* good. But it wasn't enough.

The fact of the matter was I now had a new master, and there was nothing...*nothing*...that would make me *fucking* okay with this shit.

"I thought you were in denial about all of this," she said.

"Yeah, well,"—I gave an uncomfortable laugh—"I was. I tried."

"And you've finally come to the conclusion that I'm irresistible?"

I still couldn't look at her. "I've pulled my head out of my ass and realized I want to live. And to do that, I need to keep you around."

She set her tea down on the coffee table and stood. "Great. Where shall we live? Your place or mine? Of course, I'll need to sun-proof mine, so I should probably just move in here. I'll go home and pack."

I jumped to my feet as she left her teacup on the table and headed toward the door. "Whoa. Whoa. What are you talking about?" She ignored me, trying to get past, but I stepped in front of her. Her sweet, spicy scent accosted my nose and made my mouth water. It caught me off guard and it took everything I had not to pull her into my arms and sink my teeth into her graceful throat. Clenching my jaw, I held my ground. "Where are you going?"

"Home. To pack. I already told you."

A humorless laugh burst from me. "We're not moving in together, Leeloo."

She smiled, but it was forced. "Why not? You need me. I need you. It would be easier if I was here, at your beck and call anytime of the day or night."

"What the fuck are you talking about?"

She dropped her eyes, but not before I saw the moisture welling inside of them. Crossing her arms over herself in a protective gesture, she shrugged. "I just think it would be easier."

"You don't even know me," I told her. "Why the hell are you so hellbent on shacking up with someone you barely even know?"

Her chin came up and her eyes locked on mine, still glassy with tears. "I know enough. I know you don't want to hurt me. And I know there's no escaping this mating for either of us, so why prolong the inevitable?"

"That's not exactly true," I told her. "I've dreamed of hurting you. Many, many times." Her eyes widened in surprise, but I kept going. It wasn't something I was particularly proud of, but maybe it was something she should hear. "I lay in bed during the day and imagine what it would feel like to suck you dry. *That's* how much I crave your blood."

After a moment, she asked, "What else do you dream about?"

If my confession shook her at all, she didn't show it. "Fucking you," I told her honestly. "I imagine how you taste. How you smell. How you'll feel underneath me." My eyes dropped to her feet, then slowly worked their way back to her face. And this time, I didn't bother to hide the hunger she caused. "What you look like beneath all those fancy clothes you like to wear, and how much I want to rip them off of you." I paused, wondering how much I should tell her. Then decided, fuck it. She thinks she wants to be in this with me? Then she needs to know what she's getting herself into. "I want to slap your ass with my bare palms until that pale skin is hot and pink. I want to tie you to my bed and feed from you until you're screaming for me to stop. Until your body is covered in punctures from my fangs and you're bleeding all over my bed."

She took a tiny step closer, but not like she wanted to. Like something was pulling her closer to me and she didn't even realize she'd moved. "Why do you want to do those things?"

Because it was what I craved. I didn't even try to get into the psychology of it all, although I would imagine a shrink would have a field day with me. "It doesn't matter, because it's not going to happen." I took a step back from her. *"I won't be a slave to you, Angel Moss."*

"I don't think that's--"

"That's exactly what it would be if we gave into this." I kept my voice level, but I couldn't stop the venom from lacing my words. "Except for a very brief time, I've lived my entire life, and this long-ass death, for other people. I've never been able to just be me. To do what I want to do. Live where I want to live. Hell, I couldn't even die when I wanted to, because fucking Killian needed a friend."

I slammed my mouth closed, and scrubbed my face with my hands before I dropped my arms back to my sides and gave her a level stare. "Look. Despite everything I just said, I'm not ready to die, yet. And I'm sorry I've brought you into this. I truly am. You deserve more than a life tied to a vampire as his fucking feeding bag." I paused, lowered my voice. "If I had known, I never would've taken your blood."

"I offered," she said.

"What?"

"I offered. My blood," she clarified. "I offered it to you. You didn't take anything."

"Incidentals," I told her. "The details don't matter."

"No, they do," she said. "I knew what I was doing."

Why the fuck was she fighting with me about this? "But you didn't know this was going to happen."

"Neither did you," she argued. "I mean, come on. How many other people have you drank from?"

I opened my mouth to tell her there was no way in hell I could possibly come up with a number when she cut me off.

"No. I don't want to know. I really don't." Her hands landed on her hips. "Look, Jamal. My point is, this could've happened with any of them. It just so happened that I'm the one fate chose. It is what it is. We're stuck together now. So, we might as well make the most of it."

I frowned, and somehow resisted the urge to poke around in that pretty head. Something was off here. This wasn't the witch I knew. "What's going on with you, Leeloo?"

She threw her hands in the air. "I just think it's ridiculous to act like this. The only thing we're doing is putting off the inevitable, that's all. Eventually, we're going to end up together."

"You don't know that."

"Actually, I kind of do."

Widening my stance for battle, I crossed my arms over my chest. "How?"

She looked at me like I was a few crayons short of a box. "Just look around, Jamal. Look at Killian and Lizzy, Alex and Kenya--"

"They both had a thing for their mates before the blood told them anything."

"Maybe there's a reason for that."

"And maybe it was just coincidence."

"Gods, you are so damn stubborn!"

"And you're beautiful." The words came out before I could stop them. But there was no sense taking them back. It was true, and probably the same thing she heard from any number of dudes on any given day.

However, if that was the case, she didn't show it. As a matter of fact, she appeared completely taken aback by my spontaneous statement. "You think I'm beautiful?"

I shook my head. "Don't play all innocent with me, Leeloo. I mean, look at you." I waved a hand in the air, taking in...well, everything about her. "You dye your hair bright red, never leave the house without all that makeup," I moved my hand in a circle over my face, "and you dress like you just stepped off of a runway. Obviously, you do all that to get attention. And I'm sure you succeed."

She stared at me for a long time, then she turned and sat back down on the couch. "I didn't realize you thought so little of me." As I stood there regretting my choice of words, she turned sad, hazel eyes my way. "Is that what everyone thinks? That I'm just an attention whore?"

I took a seat beside her, close enough that I could touch her if I wanted to. Probably not a good idea with the way my body was still so wound up, but I wasn't so heartless to just let her sit there alone. "I'm sorry," I told her. "That didn't come out the right way."

But she shook her head, her straight red hair brushing the bottom of her neck. "No. It's okay. I appreciate your straightforwardness."

"Angel..." I trailed off. I didn't know what to say to make this better. "Look, forget about everything I just said. Okay? The truth of it is, yeah, I think you're one of the prettiest women I've ever met. And it's not just all of this." I indicated her clothes and hair. "You've got sass, Leeloo. And you don't take any shit from anyone. Including me. I really like that about you."

"But not enough to want to be with me, huh?"

"I didn't say that."

"You don't want me to move me in here."

"Why the hell would you want to? And don't lie to me because I'll know."

I felt more than saw the way she raised her shields, and it affected me more than I'd like to admit. I didn't like her closed off to me. "You don't have to do that," I told her. "I'll stay out of your head."

She glanced at me sideways but didn't drop her shields.

"All I'm asking is that you be straight up with me, and I'll do the same."

Pressing her red lips together, she looked down at her hands. After a moment, she looked up at me. "I feel safer here, with you, than I do at home."

I frowned, completely confused as to how that could be. From what she'd told me, Angel here was one of the more powerful witches in the coven. What the hell would she need me for? Then, "Oh...the djinn."

She didn't answer, but she didn't need to. I could tell by the way she tensed up that I'd hit the nail on the head.

"What's he got on you, anyway?" It had to be something. Those things didn't just wander the earth looking for people to fuck with. There had to be some kind of connection, or a deal or something. Maybe an offense of some sort.

"I don't know."

"Don't give me that shit," I told her. "You knew he was gonna come after you. That's why you were in the cemetery trying to spell that dagger."

She was quiet for so long I thought she wasn't going to give me an answer. But at least she didn't start spouting more lies. Then she turned on the couch, bending one leg so she was facing me. Her shin pressed against the length of my thigh, and a hungry growl began in my chest. Angel froze for just a second, eyeing me, but stayed exactly as she was. "Are you okay?"

I sucked in my bottom lip as I chewed on that question for a bit. Gradually, the urge to throw her over my shoulder and take her back to my room subsided enough that I could speak. "I'm good," I told her. "Now start talking."

"Marcus, the djinn," her upper lip lifted in disgust, "has been threatening Mike's life. I need to finish the spell on the dagger if I want a chance in hell of sending him back to wherever the hell he came from."

Pure red-hot rage roiled inside of me. She was doing all this for that douche, Mike? If he was here right now, I'd rip his fucking throat out.

"Jamal?"

Fortunately for him, he wasn't here, and it gave me time to get my shit together enough to say, "So, you're doing this for fucking Mike?"

Startled eyes flew to mine. At first, she was confused, then she shook her head. "No, you don't understand. Mike hasn't done anything. He's innocent in all of this."

"I don't give a fuck what Mike may or may not have done. What the hell is he to you that you feel the need to risk your own life to protect his?" I was being irrational. But, fuck. I couldn't help it. If I didn't believe in the blood bond between us before, I sure as hell did now by the mere fact that if she hadn't been sitting here next to me, I'd be halfway to her apartment to kill Lizzy's assistant.

"Oh," she said. "Ohhh...no, you've got the wrong idea. Mike's my friend, that's it. There's nothing at all between us other than that."

"Have you fucked him?" Jesus. What the hell was wrong with me? It was none of my business what she did with her life. Or her body.

Except it was. *Because she belonged to me now.*

She made a face. "No. Of course not."

"Do you want to?"

"No," she immediately said. "Jesus, Jamal. I don't want to fuck Mike. I want to fuck you."

And just like that, the fire in my blood shifted, and all thoughts of that douche flew from my head.

18

ANGEL

"Angel..." My name was more of a growl than a spoken word, and barely discernible.

Saying what I did was the only way I could think of to distract him, and hot damn, it appeared to have worked. Not that it wasn't true. I did want to fuck him. I really, really, wanted to fuck him. And I know what he said about wanting to hurt me. I just found it hard to believe that he'd actually do anything to physically harm me. Not if we were truly mated. Wasn't there some kind of stipulation in that to keep me safe and healthy? I mean, if I'm the only food source for him now, it would make sense. And maybe that was naive of me in a way, but I was also no innocent girl. And I wasn't afraid of a little pain if the payoff meant I'd have the best orgasm of my life.

Leaning toward him until his delicious mouth was only inches from mine, I whispered, "Tell me you don't want me, and I'll back off." I was pushing this way too far, but I just couldn't go back to my place tonight. It was late, and there were too many corners on these old streets where I could be caught alone. And honestly?

I was scared shitless.

Scared the djinn was watching me, just waiting for his opportunity to finish the job he started in the cemetery. I should've brought my car, but at the time, I hadn't planned to be at the club as long as I was, and I preferred to take public transportation whenever I could. Cars were bad for the earth.

But more important than any of that, I just felt safer with Jamal around. Which was ridiculous. There wasn't anything he could do to that bastard, Marcus, that I--a witch with magic more akin to his--couldn't.

"You know I can't do that," he finally admitted. "It would be a lie."

Thank the gods. "Then why are you fighting me?"

He flashed his fangs, but instead of scaring me away, it only proved to me how much he wanted this to happen between us too, and I clenched my thighs together, trying to ease the ache between them.

Jamal twisted on the couch, leaning toward me. I expected him to kiss me again, but he didn't. Instead, he ducked his head, and I heard him take a deep inhale, then release it with a moan. I felt the scrape of one fang on the tender skin of my throat. My own breath caught in my chest as my heart began to pound. Closing my eyes, I tilted my head away to give him better access and braced myself for his bite.

"I love the scent of you." Chills ran down my spine as his deep voice rumbled against my skin. To emphasize his point, he ran the tip of his nose along the artery in my neck where my pulse fluttered rapidly. "I can smell your blood. The sunshine on your skin. And the wet heat between your legs. If I touched you right now, my fingers would come away soaked."

He wasn't wrong. "I want you to touch me." My lips parted. I couldn't get enough oxygen. Although he was so close, I could feel the heat of him through my clothes, his hands remained on his thighs. Slight brushes of his fangs and hair as he nuzzled my neck were the only contact he made. I wanted to reach for him, but I was afraid to move. Afraid to make any sudden movements because I didn't know how he'd react.

He inhaled deep, taking me into his lungs, and a shudder ran through him. "I know you do," he told me.

Yet still, he wouldn't do it. I tried to think through the haze of pure lust that was fogging my brain. What had he said earlier? He wouldn't be a slave to me. "Jamal."

"Hmmm..." His voice was deep and laced with hunger.

Slowly, I reached for his hand and brought it across both our laps, inch by careful inch. Spreading my knees apart, I pressed his palm between my legs. A hiss slithered across the skin beneath my ear, and he cupped his hand around me over my jeans. I wanted them off. I wanted us skin to skin. But I dared not move, afraid he would skitter away.

The heel of his palm pressed against my clit and a moan escaped me as I slowly, slowly, leaned back against the couch.

Opening my eyes, I found him watching me. "You don't know what you're asking of me," he whispered. His dark eyes were filled with hunger. But there was more there. There was anguish.

"All I know right now is that I feel like I'm going to burn alive from the inside out if you don't touch me." My breaths were fast and shallow, every muscle in my body tense as I fought the urge to lift my hips into his hand.

He removed his hand from between my legs and I reached for him without thinking, a cry leaving my lips. "No! Don't stop."

A laugh burst from his lips, but it didn't sound happy. "Oh, Leeloo, it's too late for that," he told me as he stood and stared down at me through eyes so dark he looked like a demon come to drag me to hell. And I must be his fallen Angel because I went with him willingly when he scooped me up from the couch and carried me back to his bedroom, setting me on my feet beside the bed.

He cursed at me as he stripped me of my boots and clothes until I was standing before him in nothing but a set of black lacy bra and panties. He tried to warn me away one last time as his hands tangled in my hair and he yanked my head back, exposing my throat so he could run his tongue along my pulse. But instead of stopping him, I slid my hands beneath his shirt, moaning when I felt his smooth skin and the ripple of muscle beneath my sensitive fingertips, a war raging within him until his big body was trembling with the effort it took him to hold himself back.

I could feel his anguish ripple through him almost as though it were my own. I heard it in the sounds he made and the way his fingers dug into my skin. He was fighting with himself. And he was losing.

With a cry of surrender, he fell to his knees before me, and my heart broke into a million little pieces as he wrapped his strong arms around my hips and pressed his lips to my stomach.

I stared down at the top of his head. I didn't understand why he felt the way he did about us, but I knew I didn't want him like this. Broken and weak. "Stop," I told him. "Jamal! Stop!"

Immediately, he froze, pressing his forehead to my womb, his nose against my sex and his chest heaving. "What's wrong?" he asked.

"I just..." What? I can't stand the thought of you suffering like this? I held his head against me, fighting a battle of my own as I tried to get myself under control. My breasts felt heavy and swollen, my legs shook, and it took everything I had not to press his mouth against my pussy and beg him to ease the ache there with his tongue. The thing was though, through our bond or whatever, I felt the way every single cell in his body tried to resist what he was doing, and yet no matter how he fought it, he couldn't keep himself away from me. His instincts weren't giving him a choice.

He had no choice.

That's it! That's what he needed. It had to be his choice. Not mine. Not the gods. Not the mating bond. HIS.

Now how did I do that?

"I just...just no. I changed my mind." Taking my hands off his head, I let them fall to my sides. I would've stepped away from him if his arms weren't still wrapped around my hips and thighs.

I felt more than heard him laugh. "You're lying."

"I'm not." And I wasn't. I didn't want him like this. Even if he got into my head, he would see it was the truth. Blood bond or not, I couldn't in good conscience force him into being with me. He had to want it, too. It was the only way he would accept it. "I mean it, Jamal." And then I waited.

After a few moments, his arms fell away from me slowly, his palms sliding down the backs of my legs all the way to my ankles before he let go. His head lifted, and he sat back on his heels, his dark eyes on the "V" between my legs for several heartbeats before they traveled up my torso, lingering on my lace covered breasts before finally making it to my face. His upper lip lifted in a snarl, flashing his fangs, and his tone was mocking when he said, "You changed your mind."

I took a deep breath, hoping my instincts about this were right. "Yes."

He looked past me, rubbing his chin. But I wasn't fooled. This male might appear all calm and collected, but I knew otherwise, even if I couldn't feel the tension between us. Then he nodded, and suddenly he was on his feet. "Fine. Get the fuck out."

"What?" Wait. This wasn't the way it was supposed to go.

"Get out," he repeated. "I'm not sure what part of that sentence you don't understand."

Oh, I understood all right. He was hurt, whether he would admit it to himself or not, and he was being an asshole. But that's okay. Let him sulk about it for a while. It would only strengthen my plan. Bending down, I grabbed my clothes and shoes off the floor and held them in front of me. "I'm sorry," I told him. "I just need a little time. And I think you do, too."

"Mmm-hmm." He wouldn't look at me.

Walking around him, I rushed toward the doors in nothing but my underwear. It was cold outside, but I needed to get out of there. Jamal was hungry, and not just for sex. I could tell because he was tracking me again, and because my blood was singing in response. The same as my body. And if I didn't leave now, if he caught me, I wouldn't be able to stop him again and my big show here would all be for naught.

I'd almost made it to the door when he was there, blocking my path. Nothing but a slight breeze passing my right side had given me any indication he'd moved. I pulled up short, just barely squelching my cry of surprise. "Let me pass."

Jamal's eyes traveled over my face then dropped down to the clothes and shoes hugged against my chest. His head slowly cocked to the side and his eyes narrowed. He looked angry. "You're not walking outside like that."

I lifted one eyebrow. "Please. I've worn much more revealing stuff at the beach." I meant it as a "come on, dude, don't be a douche" comment, something to lighten the mood, but it only seemed to anger him more. I actually heard his teeth click together he clenched his jaw so hard. "I just want to go," I told him.

He took a step toward me. "You're not going anywhere, Leeloo."

I'm not? Well, okay then. It seemed my plan was working. But I couldn't make it too easy on him. "Step aside, Jamal. I want to go home."

"Why don't you make me?"

He stood before me, a challenge in his eyes. Did he know the game I was playing? I couldn't tell for sure, but either way, I had to make it look good.

"I'm not gonna warn you again," I told him.

His answer was to take another step until he was so close, I could touch him just by lifting one of my fingers.

I reached deep into my emotions and brought all of the frustration and anger and fear I was feeling toward the djinn to the surface. My lips moved as I muttered a quick spell, calling to the natural energy surrounding us to help me. Then I lifted one hand and swiped it through the air.

The look of surprise on his face was priceless as Jamal was lifted from his feet and thrown into the kitchen counter.

Quickly, I rushed to the patio doors. But I'd barely made it a few feet when I heard a predatory growl that lifted every hair on my body and sent tingles of warning down my spine...

19

BROGAN

What the hell was she doing here?

Again?

High-fiving my man, Jamal, I jogged off the stage and went straight to the men's room to shower and change. My plan was to sneak out the back door and haul my happy ass home before she could corner me.

Again.

Esme, the woman waiting for me, had started out as a sweet piece of ass who smelled really good and ended up as a pain in the ass who asked waaayyy too many questions. And I was stupid enough to answer entirely too many of them before I realized what she was doing. But, ya know, I've always been a sucker for Latin girls. Dark hair, dark eyes that could see all the way down to your soul, golden brown skin, passion and trouble. Mmm, mmm, mmmm. That's what those girls were made of, and this one was no different. I palmed my sex just thinking about her.

All that being said, I'd never fed from her. Not that I hadn't tried. I grunted to the room in general as I remembered the way she'd ever so politely refused my invitation to join me in the back room for a private dance. I'd even offered to give it to her for free--so to speak. But she'd told me she wasn't interested in that.

However, ever since then, she'd shown up at least once or twice a week. Always when I was working. And after the first few times, I stopped inviting her into the back room. But when I danced, I danced for her and her alone.

We didn't talk anymore. Not until the night I'd stayed behind to walk Kenya home and found Esme waiting for me outside the club. It had been stupid of me to listen to her when she'd told me she could make it home fine on her own, but the look on Esme's face...I thought something had happened, and I was worried about her. Turns out my instincts had been right.

She had that same look on her face tonight, but I wasn't falling for it this time. That woman and her life was of no concern to me. I needed to stay out of all of it, stay away from her and her questions before she discovered more than she needed to know.

I was done with my shower in record time and didn't even bother buttoning my shirt (my favorite one. It had hula girls dancing all over it) or lacing my boots. Shoving my G-string in my jeans pocket to throw in the wash when I got home, I carefully opened the door, half expecting Esme to be waiting for me in the hall. When I didn't see her, I tiptoed down the hall to the back door, and, with a quick look over my shoulder, shoved it open. Grinning, I let it slam behind me and walked out into the alley.

"Not hanging around tonight, Brogan?"

"Jesus fucking Christ!" My fangs shot down and I swung around, snapping my mouth shut just in time. I even managed not to wince as one razor sharp fang sliced the inside of my bottom lip on the way down.

The woman in the alleyway laughed.

She fucking laughed.

And I guess she had the right. Somehow, she'd managed to sneak up on a fucking vampire and scare the bejesus out of him. A feat not many humans could claim. Well, so much for my sneaking out of there.

"Are you scared of me or something?"

"Pfft." I wasn't even going to dignify that question with an answer. The woman had no idea. "What do you want, Esme?"

She glanced around the alley, giving me a minute to admire her in all her gorgeousness. Tonight, she was wearing black jeans that hugged her thick curves like a second skin, a red blouse, and a short, black leather jacket. Her lips were painted red, too. But the rest of her makeup was minimal as far as I could tell. Of course, I am a guy. So there's no telling what I was actually looking at here. Long hair, so dark it was almost black, hung in thick waves over one shoulder, tied that way with a ponytail holder.

"Wanna go get something to eat?"

Although her expression was completely innocent, I knew damn well what she was doing. And I gave her my standard answer. "You know damn well I don't date customers. I've told you this plenty of times."

"It's not a date," she said. "It's dinner. I never asked you to buy."

Tenacious. Did I say before how Latin women were tenacious? "It's not happening. I have things to do."

"I'll come with you. Keep you company." She smiled a wide smile, all white teeth and dimples, and my heart stuttered to a stop.

I managed to shake my head. "I didn't ask for company."

Smile still in place, like she knew how it made me stupid, she walked up beside me and laced her arm through mine. I had to give her credit. The woman had balls. Most humans had a sixth sense about me and would keep their distance. Unless, of course, I turned on my vampire charm. Then they were drawn to me like they hadn't had water in days and I was the only oasis in the desert.

But not this one.

I started to button up my shirt. "Esme, I told you I didn't want company."

"Well, I do. So, you're stuck with me. You might as well just deal with it and let's get on about things. I don't want to be up all night. I have an early meeting."

"Tomorrow's Sunday."

She looked at me as if to say, "And?"

I looked down at her. She only came up just past my shoulder in heels, a tiny thing with an ass that would make a man weep watching it walk away, and an attitude the size of The Rock. "Fine." I told her.

If anything, that smile got even brighter.

We walked out of the alley and I headed toward the closest restaurant. No sense in dragging this out.

Despite the colder weather, the streets were crowded with people full of the holiday spirit. As I walked through them with this gorgeous woman on my arm, I held my chin high and tried to ignore the sense of pride that filled my chest. Esme wasn't mine. Hell, she didn't even want me. Like every other time I'd taken her out, she was only doing this to try to get information out of me.

And she already knew too much.

20

JAMAL

What the fuck kind of game was this witch trying to play with me? Did she get off on coming on strong like she did, breaking down every fucking defense I had until I was *literally* on my fucking knees for her, only to think she could walk the fuck out on me?

Yeah. That ain't happening.

But none of this seemed right. Leeloo liked to play, I already knew that about her, but I've always had the impression she was too straight up for this kind of shit. She wouldn't fuck with me. Not like this. Witch or not, I didn't get that vibe from her.

So what was it? Was she scared of me? Good. She should be. But I didn't think that was it, either. Especially since she just pranced out of my bedroom without even checking over her shoulder to see if I was following her. Nah, she wasn't scared of me. Plus, we both knew she could keep me off of her if she really wanted to.

Like she'd just proven to me again.

When she'd thrown me away from her and my hip rammed into my kitchen counter, all coherent thought fled my mind. The next thing I knew I was back in my bedroom slamming Angel down onto the mattress and getting her beneath me. My hand was around her throat and my hips pressed her into the bed before either of us realized what was happening. As I stared down at her, I didn't know what I craved more--her blood or her pussy--but tonight, I was going to have both.

With my mind, I turned on the bedside lamp. I didn't need it. I was a predator. My night vision was excellent. But I wanted her to see me. See the male she now belonged to, see what she had started and what I was about to finish.

Once her mind caught up with where we were, she pressed against my shoulders, trying to push me off, and when I got tired of it, I gathered her wrists in my free hand and raised them above her head. The movement made her back arch and pushed her breasts into my chest. My eyes greedily took in the sight of her pale body pressed against mine. The poor excuse for a bra she wore barely covered her nipples, but it was still too much. I needed her naked so I could feast on all those delicious curves she somehow managed to keep hidden beneath her fancy clothes. And if she was nice to me, I'd make her come while I did it. "You're not going anywhere. Do you get me?"

Wide eyes met mine. I don't know if she understood what I said or not. My throat felt like I'd swallowed a handful of razor blades and my body pulsed with every beat of my heart, my cock so swollen the zipper of my jeans dug into the tender skin. Moving my hand up to her jaw, I forced her to look away, exposing her throat to me, and my eyes locked onto the artery throbbing just beneath the near translucent skin. Rearing back, I opened my mouth and struck, excitement streaking through me when she cried out in surprise and pain.

Warm, sweet spice filled my mouth. The taste so perfectly exquisite hot pleasure slid down my spine and tightened my balls, and I had to concentrate hard so as not to come in my pants. Her blood slid down the back of my throat, soothing my thirst but not satiating it. Not by a long shot. It warmed my chest as it went down, like strong liquor, then shot out like a stick of dynamite had just exploded in my gut, feeding my cells with an addictive pulse of electricity I could never describe accurately enough so someone else would understand it. I moaned as it hit me, only realizing just then how much I'd craved this since the night at the cemetery. How much I'd needed it.

How much I needed her.

Licking the puncture wounds closed to help them heal, I lifted my weight from her and released her wrists. She immediately slapped one hand over her throat where I'd just fed, pulling it away and staring at her fingers in surprise when she saw no blood. "What the fuck, Jamal?! Let me up."

She bucked her hips, trying to throw me off. And when that didn't work, she tried to wiggle out from under me.

I grabbed the front of her bra and ripped it apart, exposing her breasts to my hungry gaze. They were full and lush, so pale I could see the tiny blue veins throughout, and topped with hardened, dusty-pink nipples that were just begging to be touched.

But then I looked closer.

Red marks marred her perfect skin where the underwires from her bra had dug into the sides of her skin. Pure rage that anything would hurt her, even something self-inflicted, tore through me, and I pulled the lace the rest of the way off her and threw the stupid thing as far as I could. Later, I would burn it.

Angel wrapped her arms around herself, trying to cover up her nakedness. She watched as her bra landed on the floor, mouth hanging open in disbelief. "Do you know how much that thing cost?"

I didn't give a shit. I'd buy her twenty more. Comfortable bras that didn't cut into her skin. Or better yet, I would destroy them all. I'd much prefer she didn't wear them anyway. Pushing her hands out of the way, I cupped her breasts in my hands and massaged the tender, damaged skin.

"What are you doing? Jamal? Please talk to me."

I heard the nervous tremor in her voice, but all I could bring myself to say was, "You're not leaving." Then I pushed her back onto the bed and bent over her, laving the angry red marks with my tongue before making my way to her nipple. Taking it between my teeth, I teased the tip with my tongue, first one then the other, until my witch was panting and writhing on the bed. Her fingers were wrapped around my arms, braced on either side of her, but I didn't feel the way her nails dug into my skin. The only thing that had my full attention was how good she tasted and how perfect she felt beneath me.

When she asked me to stop, I pressed my hardened sex between her thighs. When she started to beg, I sank my fangs into the lushest part of the inside of her breast and drank deep, my fingers playing with the tip of her opposite breast as I worked one thigh between hers and pushed her legs apart until she was open to me and I could settle my hips between them. Sliding one hand between us, I ripped the thin piece of lace that covered one hip, then the other, and the whisper of material fell to the mattress, leaving her bare and exposed beneath me.

I didn't bother closing the wound open on her breast, it wasn't bleeding much, and I made my way down her body, kissing and biting her in turn, until she was covered with the punctures from my fangs. But as much as she protested, her tone lacked conviction and her body told me the truth. The way her hips lifted to my mouth and her hands held my head between her legs. The way she was soaking wet when I pushed apart her folds with my tongue. And how she sucked in a breath when I found the sensitive bud near the top swollen and ready for me.

And how she came apart almost immediately, crying out my name and shuddering beneath my hands as she soaked my tongue.

Sitting up, I grabbed the bottom of my shirt and yanked it off, my shoes and jeans following. Next time, I would play. For now, the only thing I wanted was to be inside of my witch. She watched me with eyes hazed in pleasure as I came down over her, one hand gripping the base of my cock. Lining up the head with her entrance, I slid inside. She was hot and tight and wet, and my eyes nearly rolled back in my head as she took me all the way in.

I pulled out and pushed back in, hooking one arm beneath her knee so I could get even deeper. I watched as she threw her head back, that red hair spread all over my black comforter, her sweet lips open on a sound of pleasure, and a possessive growl rumbled in my chest.

"Drink from me."

Her eyes flew open and clashed with mine. I'd never seen anything so beautiful as the way the greens and golds and browns mixed and changed, like one of those kid's toys, or a star bursting into existence.

"Drink from me," I growled as my hips moved slowly, in and out, my cock so hard I felt like I was about to burst from my skin.

She moaned as I fucked her, and her eyes travelled over my face and throat, searching for how the hell she was supposed to do that. Wrapping the leg I was holding around my hip, I cupped the back of her head and pulled her mouth to the side of my neck. "Bite," I ordered. "Hard."

The hairs on the back of my neck lifted as she murmured something against my skin and magic swirled around us, and then I felt the sharp edges of her teeth. "Yes, baby. Do it." There was pressure, and then I felt the resistance give as she bit through the skin with a little help from the spell she'd cast. Her sweet lips latched onto me, and she began to suck.

Holy fucking shit.

Her moans were lost somewhere beneath my own shout as I came harder than I ever had in my life, my hips slamming my cock into her over and over, filling her with my come as my blood filled her mouth. I was still jerking inside of her when I lifted her wrist to my mouth and bared my fangs. Her arm jerked as I bit her, not as gently as I could have, and then she was convulsing beneath me, her body squeezing my semi-hard cock as she came all over me.

MINE.

The word reverberated through my head, hell, through my entire being. I was a fool to think I could've denied it. I'd been drawn to Leeloo since the first time I'd ever seen her. Only my own stubbornness had kept me away this long.

A long time later, we lay wrapped around each other, our hearts beating in time with each other, both of us still revved up on blood and sex. Brushing her hair from her face, I dropped kisses on her forehead, her nose, her luscious lips. Angel smiled, her eyes fluttering open to meet mine, and my own smile faltered.

She stared up at me, all of the emotions she was feeling flowing through me along with her blood. And that was when I felt it.

The triumph.

It was subtle. She was trying to hide it, to bury it beneath the affection and satisfaction and lust, but it was there. Without warning, I dipped into her mind. It was a lot easier now with the blood bond.

"Son of a bitch." I flashed my fangs at her with a hiss of warning, then pushed myself off the bed and grabbed my jeans. I just heard everything I needed to hear.

I'd moved so fast it took her a second to find me in the room, and when she did, she sat up in alarm. "What's wrong? What's happened?"

"Get out," I told her.

"What? Jamal..."

"You think this is a fucking game, Leeloo? Huh?"

Confusion and panic were written all over her face, but she got up and started to get dressed. "Jamal, what are you fucking talking about?"

"What am I fucking talking about?" I was so angry I didn't know how I didn't have my hands around her throat again. "Was this your plan all along? Did you know somehow?"

She stopped moving with her shirt on and jeans unzipped and threw her hands in the air. "I don't know what you're fucking talking about!"

"Did. You. KNOW?" I shouted. "About us? Did you know about us?"

"What? No! How the hell would I have known?"

I didn't believe her. Dismissing her with a wave of my hand, I left the room.

"Jamal!" One boot on and one still in her hand, she followed me. "Jamal, please! Let me explain."

"Explain what?" I snarled. "That you had this planned all along?"

"No! I..." She ran a hand through her mussed hair, and when she looked up at me again, there were tears in her eyes. "Jamal..."

But I shook my head. "You're smart, Leeloo. I'll give you that much. You played me just right. Knew exactly how to get me to do what you wanted me to." I'd never felt such pain as I did right now. Such betrayal. Not from Killian. Not from anyone. My fucking bones ached with it. I couldn't even look at her.

"I just...it had to be your choice," she said quietly.

"But it wasn't," I told her as I stared at the floor. "It was never my choice." Walking over to the doors, I pulled it open. Leaving it that way, I walked past her and went back to my room, slamming the door behind me.

Her sobbing cry was a nice touch as she walked out.

21

ANGEL

How could I have miscalculated that so awesomely?

A little over a week had gone by since the night I spent at Jamal's, and I was still trying to figure out how he'd figured me out. I tried to go by The Purple Fang a few times, but was denied access at the door. I'd left quietly each time without causing a ruckus. It was probably better if I didn't force my way in there. I'm not sure I'd want to see what was surely going on. At least I knew he couldn't feed from anyone else, so, eventually, he would have to come back to me. Right?

Having Mike still at my place didn't do me any favors. The night Jamal had kicked me out, I'd run home and spilled my heart out to him. I knew Mike had a thing for me, but I was confident our friendship would be more important.

I was wrong.

Mike listened without interruption when I told him everything that happened, from Jamal saving me in the cemetery to the way things had been left between us. He didn't console me or berate me for trying to trick him into accepting our mating. As a matter of fact, he didn't say anything at all. He just made a sound of disbelief and went back to the couch, refusing to talk to me. Although later that day he did break his vow of silence long enough to tell me to let him know as soon as the threat of the djinn was taken care of and he could leave.

The only one who would talk to me was Lizzy. And even though I'd never gone out of my way to be friendly with her, I was beginning to think maybe I'd misjudged her after all.

"So, Aunt Judy and the rest of the gang are coming back today?" she asked.

We were at Ancient Magicks, the place I'd stolen the dagger from. The dagger that was now hidden in my apartment. Although she wouldn't know that. I don't think she ever goes into the secret room in the back unless she's forced to. I'd brought her a coffee and a pup cup for her old dog, Wiggles. Bending down, I held it for him while he lapped up the whipped cream. "Last I knew," I told her. "No one has called or anything to tell me otherwise."

She stopped counting out her cash for the till and gave me a strange look.

"What?" I asked her, then patted Wiggles on his little black head and threw away his empty cup.

"They haven't called you? Like, not even to update you on what's happening with the Seattle coven or anything?"

"Nope." I tried to play it off like this was a normal thing, even though it totally wasn't. My aunt always checked in when she was out of town. But I knew they were okay because I knew from Lizzy that Alex was checking in with Kenya a few times a day, but if he was telling her anything, she hadn't said.

So that left me with the only possible reason no one had been in touch with me, and I didn't have to be a mind reader to figure this out.

They know.

"You don't think that's odd?"

One arm wrapped around my middle, I chewed my thumbnail and stared out the window of her shop. Tourists strolled by, drinks in hand and decorated with beads for the holiday. It was only late morning and it was already a balmy day. The temperature was supposed to reach the high sixties by that afternoon.

"Angel?" Lizzy called my name loud enough that I got the impression it wasn't the first time she'd done it. "What's wrong?"

Despite the fact I was wearing thick leggings, flats with socks, and a long sweater, I couldn't stop the shivering that started somewhere in my gut and spread out to the rest of my body. "I have to tell you something," I whispered.

Glancing at a group of people who were peering into the display window, Lizzy took my arm and pulled me behind the curtain that separated the storage room from the rest of the shop. When we were out of sight of the general public, she turned toward me. "What's going on? What's wrong? If this is about Jamal, he'll come around--"

I cut her off with a wave of my hand. "No. This isn't about him. Except for the fact that he's going to hate me even more than he already does when he finds out."

"I don't understand."

Looking at my newly discovered cousin, dark eyes filled with concern--concern for *me*, someone who's been a complete bitch to her most of the time--I lost what little control I'd been keeping over my emotions. "It's all my fault," I cried as the tears I'd been holding in for what seemed like a lifetime spilled over and flowed down my face.

"What is?"

"Everything! Kenya almost dying...Alex almost dying...everything!" And then I burst into tears.

Ducking out of the room for a moment, Lizzy showed back up with a box of tissues and handed me one, which I gratefully took from her. Wiping my face and blowing my nose, I tried to get my shit together enough to tell her.

"It's okay," she said. "Take your time. The customers can wait."

"I can't talk here..."

Grabbing my hand, she pulled me to the back corner of the storage room and moved the rolling shelves out of the way. "Open it," she told me, indicating the hidden door. "This room is spelled, right? No one will hear us."

I chanted the spell to open the door and went inside with her. With a wave of my hand, I lit the candles placed throughout the stone room. The misery I'd been holding at bay for all of these months burst from me like water bursting through a dam. "It's my fault he's here, Lizzy."

"Who?"

By the way she was looking at me, I think she knew. But I told her anyway. "The djinn. Marcus."

She took a step back, but to her credit, she didn't completely freak out and even managed to keep her voice level when she demanded, "Tell me exactly what you're talking about, Angel."

So, I did. I told her everything. How I'd met him in a bar one night long before she moved here when I was feeling really down and frustrated. How I knew right away what he was, or at least I knew what he wasn't…and that was a normal human. Or even a witch. No, he was more. Much more. But instead of making my excuses and getting the hell out of there to warn the coven he was here in our city, I ordered another drink.

I listened while he gave me his sob story, telling me about his brother's betrayal and death, and how he was looking for what little family he had left. The offspring of his brother and the woman they both loved. What he didn't bother to tell me was how many generations had passed since that had happened, or why he wanted to find them.

And me, in my inebriated state, had opened my mouth and told him everything. About me. The coven. And the vampires we shared the city with. I didn't notice how his interest perked up when I mentioned Alice and Alex. Didn't think it strange when he ran into me on the street the next day.

Full of righteous anger on how I perceived the way the coven and mostly my aunt, the high priestess, had been treating me, I'd allowed him to sweet-talk me. I fell completely for his charm, and I agreed to help him. He wasn't asking much, not really. Just some more information on his niece and nephew and maybe some updates here and there so that perhaps, someday, they could reconnect.

It was a relatively harmless way to stick it to my coven without actually doing a lot of damage. Or so I'd thought.

And then he started asking more and more of me. And when I refused the first time, Kenya got sick. I'd just about talked myself into telling Aunt Judy I knew who had done it. Telling her everything. "But then we saved her. Well, Alex did. And then she and Alex were taken and...well...you know the rest."

Lizzy stared at me for a long time. "What are you not telling me?"

I took a deep breath. I'd gone this far, might as well keep on going. "The reason Mike has been so MIA isn't because he's sick, or flakey, or just a bad employee. He's at my place."

"But you told us you haven't seen him..."

"I lied. He's been staying at my place because Marcus is using him to keep me in line. He has some kind of magical fist around Mike's heart, and he threatens to make it burst in his chest if I don't do what he asks." I pressed my hands to either side of my face and started to pace. "I don't know what to do, I don't know what to do, I don't know what to do..."

"Okay, okay. Calm down," she told me. "Let's just think about this."

"It's too late, Lizzy."

She threw her hands out in front of her, palms out. "No. No. We can fix this." One hand on her hip, the other pushed a strand of dark hair behind her ear. "We have to tell Aunt Judy. We have to tell the coven."

My stomach fell. I knew it was the right move, but it was too late. I could feel it in my bones. There was no running to the high priestess and explaining everything to her and begging her forgiveness. Things had gone too far. I'd let them get too far. And besides...

"She already knows," I told her. "They already know."

Lizzy's brown eyes met mine, full of fear for me, as my cell phone buzzed in my pocket. My eyes never leaving hers, I pulled it out and answered it.

"Hello, Aunt Judy."

22

•

JAMAL

A flash of red caught my eye and I stopped dead in the middle of the sidewalk, my head whipping around. But it was nothing, just a ribbon fluttering through the air that someone had dropped from a balcony.

It was only a few days before Christmas, and I decided to go walk around a bit instead of hanging around the house. As he did every year, Killian had opened the house for tourists so they could come in and gawk at the historical architecture and numerous decorated trees throughout. Normally, it was kind of amusing, and I would hang out to watch the show. But tonight, I just couldn't get into the spirit.

It wasn't because I was hungry, although strangely enough, I was. Which was odd. I'd been a vampire long enough that I really didn't need to feed that often anymore. But I'd felt on edge all week, ever since the night after I kicked Angel out of my place. I just...I fucking craved her. Her blood. Her body. Hell, even just the sound of her voice and the smell of her red hair. So, when I thought I saw that hair just now every single fucking cell in my body had jumped to attention, and then came crashing right back down again when I figured out it wasn't her.

So, yeah. I just wasn't in the fucking mood.

The humans were giving me strange looks as I stood there, the crowds parting around me like water around a rock. I cursed softly and continued on my way home. The showings should be done by now, and I really had nowhere else to go.

As I walked, the voices of the carolers in Jackson Square rose over the chatter of the tourists. I heard Christmas bells somewhere, and the snort of a horse. The air was thick with the smell of bodies and alcohol and sewage, although not as bad as it was in the summer months. And all of that was doused in a good dose of Cajun cooking.

All these little things I never took the time to notice anymore followed me as I made my way back to the house. Not for the first time, I wished The Fang was open tonight. I could've really used the escape I got on stage. Not for the attention, but just to forget...

I was half a block away from the house when I heard voices gathered in the courtyard. Hurrying now, I opened the gate and let myself in, curious to see what was happening. All eyes turned to me when I walked into the light from the gas lanterns. "What's going on?" I asked them. They were all there: Killian, Lizzy, Kenya, Alex, Elias, Dae-Jung, and Brogan.

It was Alex, Kenya's mate, who came forward. "My coven is meeting tonight out in the swamps."

Okay. Not sure why that was a big deal. The witch coven did weird shit like that sometimes. "And you wanted to use our house, or...?"

"He doesn't know," Lizzy told him before turning anxious eyes to me.

Something began to creep along my skin. Not magic. Something else. My instincts giving me a warning. "What don't I know?" I directed the question to Killian, knowing he'd be straight up with me and wouldn't try to spare my feelings. It's the kind of relationship we had. The same one we'd had right from the beginning when I'd stumbled up to him in the dead of night, bloody and starving and on the run from my first master, the slave owner who'd bought me. Killian had just been a kid, as was I, and the first words out of his mouth were, *You're probably not going to live long enough to get free. You understand?*

Only thanks to him and many others, I did make it, and I did live free, for what it was worth, until Killian found me again and became my new master. He was honest about that, too, as much as I hated it. So he was the one I turned to to tell me what was happening.

"They have Angel," he said, his Irish accent thick with some emotion I couldn't read. "She's the reason the djinn is here.

The reason he got to Kenya and Alex. She's the one who helped him escape."

I held up my hand. "What are you fucking talking about?"

Exchanging a glance with Lizzy, he came closer, lowering his voice. "She never said anything to you, then? Never gave any indication she was involved?"

What the fuck was he talking about? I searched his face. "No. I haven't spent that much time with her. And the one night we were together...we weren't exactly talking a lot." I looked around at everyone else, not knowing what to think, but wondering if they'd somehow made a mistake. "I never got the impression she would do something like that." But would I really be surprised? She tricked me into fucking her, into giving her my blood...

The corner of Killian's mouth lifted in a half smile, but only briefly before he became serious again. "Angel confessed all of this to Lizzy today. The djinn got a hold of her in a bad moment, and at first she only agreed to give him some information--"

"About Alice." I remembered what Kenya had told us about his fascination with her as a direct descendent of a woman he'd once known.

"And me," Alex chimed in.

I gave him a look. "Nobody's talking to you."

"Hey!" Kenya stepped up in front of him and stuck her finger in my face. "Don't talk to him like that. You're upset, but don't go taking it out on Alex."

"It's okay, honey."

"No," she told her mate. "It's not okay."

I paced away. I was done with this conversation. "I don't know what the hell you all think you're doing here, anyway. What?" I threw my arms wide. "What the fuck is this? Some kind of fucking intervention? What the hell do you want me to do?" I glared at them all. "Fate gave me a fucking bitch for a mate. I'm sorry. I don't know why you're telling me all this. I haven't even seen her in a week. Hell, I don't even fucking want her, so what the fuck do I care?"

A stinging pain on my cheek, and my head whipped hard to the right. My fangs shot down and I hissed in warning as I turned to see who the hell had the balls to hit me.

Lizzy stood in front of me, her hands clenched into fists at her sides like she was trying to hold herself back from striking me again. "We expect you to *fucking* help her, you asshole."

I stuck my face in hers, my upper lip lifted in a sneer. "Why the hell would I do that?"

A nanosecond later, a growl of rage ripped through the courtyard, and I was flying through the air, not stopping until my back slammed into the cast iron bars behind me. I landed on my feet, only to be shoved right back against the fence.

Killian bared his fangs at me. "Don't you EVER talk to her like that again." Though his voice was low enough so as not to attract unwanted attention from the humans on the street, the threat was very, very real.

However, I couldn't bring myself to give a shit. "The witches are about to string up my mate?" I hissed. "Great. Let them. Maybe now I can be done with her. Done with all of you."

Killian's dark golden eyes began to glow and he flashed his fangs. "Is that what you truly want, Jamal? You want to die, then? Because that's exactly what will happen if anything happens to Angel. I don't know why she did what she did, and I'm sure as hell not happy about it, but this is your mate. Don't you think you owe it to her to hear what she has to say? Or at the very least just try to keep her alive? Because you might feel fine now. But a time will come, and that time will be soon, that you're going to need to feed, and you're going to need her for that."

I stared straight at him, but didn't say a word. He just didn't get it. None of them did.

Killian stepped back with a sound of disbelief. "This is how you're going to play it, then? Fine. If that's really what you want, ya bastard, I can help you out with that. Right here. Right now. Because I'm sick to death of all your whining." He stepped into me, his power swirling around me and shoving me back into the bars. "I SAVED YOUR FUCKING LIFE! Twice!! And all I've gotten out of it is *years* and *years* of you acting like I've offended you somehow. Like I did you no favors at all. Or myself, for that matter."

He stood before me full of his righteous rage, and I snapped. "I NEVER ASKED YOU TO SAVE ME," I screamed back at him. "I never wanted any of this!"

"As we can tell from the way you refuse to become a part of this family! Living out here in the guest house like a stranger! Barely talking to me. The only time I see you anymore is at The Fang!"

"I never wanted this family," I told him. "*You* wanted this family."

"Jesus fucking shite." The disgust in his voice matched the expression on his face. It hurt to see him looking at me this way. More than I thought it would. But I couldn't take it back.

"I should've left you in that fucking ditch." He stared at me for a long time, so many emotions reflecting back at me I couldn't keep track of them, then he turned and walked away. "Die then," he called over his shoulder. "I'm done with this fucking shite. I'm done with *you*, Jamal."

We all watched him walk to the back door and go inside. He didn't even slam the door. He left it wide open.

"Why do you have to do this to him?" Lizzy asked. "He loves you." Then she followed him inside.

Gradually, the others followed, some casting glances my way, but no one else said anything. The air turned heavy around me, like I was watching a funeral progression.

And I guess I kind of was. My own.

I stood there for what seemed like a long time, my thoughts going a mile a minute and in no way keeping up with everything I was feeling. Rage, relief, sorrow, fear, loss...it formed a funnel of emotions inside of me like some kind of sick tornado. It gathered strength, growing larger and larger, until it took up all of the space inside me and I couldn't draw air into my lungs and my heart felt like it was being squeezed by a giant fist. Still, it grew. It grew until I couldn't hold it in anymore and I threw my head back and released it with a roar that shook me to my bones as I fell to my knees on the brick pavement.

Even when I could breathe again and my heart resumed beating, I didn't have it in me to get up. I don't know how long I stayed like that before two pairs of feet appeared in front of me, both wearing black boots.

"I don't know how long you plan to stay down there feeling sorry for yourself," Kenya told me. "But I'm going with Alex to try to save Angel. If you decide you want to get up and come help your mate like any real male would, you're welcome to ride with us."

"You have two minutes," Alex said. "We'll wait in the car."

Walking around me, they went out through the gate.

Son of a fucking bitch.

I closed my eyes. I just wanted it to be over. Wanted to forget this life and everyone in it. The things I'd been through were things no man, woman, or child should ever have had to endure. I just wanted to forget...

I'm sorry.

My head rose and my eyes darted around the empty courtyard, and it was only then I realized there were tears clouding my vision. I wiped them away with my forearm and looked again. I'd heard the words as clearly as if she was standing right in front of me.

I'm so sorry...

My fangs ached to slice through skin and my blood began to burn as it raced through my veins. Hazel green eyes filled my vision, sad, afraid, and yet accepting of what was about to happen.

"Leeloo?" I was on my feet, driven by instinct, before my mind could catch up to my actions.

Jamal...

"No!" I was running now. Afraid I wouldn't make it on time. I didn't stop to think what I was doing, or why. All I knew was there was this force inside of me urging me to get to her. "Hang on, Leeloo," I said out loud. "I'm coming."

"Jamal! Get in!"

A dark blue Jeep with an open top slowed down beside me and I looked over to see Kenya waving me over. With a glance around to make sure no one was watching, I followed them, cutting across the intersection and jumping into the back. "Get me to her."

"On our way," Alex answered.

As he maneuvered through The Quarter and out toward the swamplands, I kept a tight grip on the invisible bond between my blood and Angel's, and hoped she could feel it, too.

23

ANGEL

I'd been ordered to meet the coven at an undisclosed location far outside of the city. And if I hadn't already been positive they knew what I'd done, that right there would've told me. There was only one reason the coven ever met away from civilization, and it hadn't happened since before my time.

To rid the coven of a dangerous member.

And that member was me.

I couldn't run. I couldn't hide. That order was magically enforced. If I tried to leave the area, they would find me and haul my ass right back to the city, so there was really no sense in it. All I could do was confess what I'd already told Lizzy and beg for their forgiveness.

My hands were gripped so tight on the steering wheel my knuckles were white and I wasn't sure if Mike would be able to pry them off. I'd brought him with me, hoping the coven could help him once they were done with me. I hadn't told him what was happening, only that we were performing a special ceremony. I don't know if he believed me. He'd been especially quiet ever since we'd left the apartment. Maybe he could feel something wasn't right and was afraid to ask me.

When we arrived at the clearing, I didn't get out right away. Neither did Mike. I felt him staring at me, but I couldn't look at him. I couldn't do anything but sit there with my hands still wrapped around the steering wheel.

I inhaled deep and released it, slow and steady.

The coven stood in a semi-circle around a small fire, one end open for me to step through, then they would close it around me. I knew how this worked. I would be tried, judged, and convicted, and I deserved all of it. The only thing I didn't know was what my punishment would be. I guess I should be glad I didn't see a stake with logs piled up around it.

"Okay," I told Mike. "Let's go. And whatever happens"—I met his eyes—"don't cause a scene. We don't want to piss anyone off any more than they already are."

"So, they know," he said. "That's what you haven't been telling me. They know about your deal with the djinn."

I turned my head, staring at my coven. My family. "They do."

"Fuck."

But I shook my head. "No. I deserve whatever they're about to throw at me. And maybe they can help you. If I wasn't such a fucking coward..." I swallowed hard. "I should've just told them everything from the start, before I got in so deep." Reaching over, I took his hand. "They'll help you. You're innocent in all of this."

"I hope so."

It wasn't until I got out of the car that I noticed the others standing off to the side in the shadows. The warlock with the raven, his vampire mate, and two others, Luukas and Keira--the master vampire from Seattle and his powerful witch. I'd only met them that one time at The Purple Fang when they came down to help us save Alex and Kenya, after which I'd stayed far away, too afraid they would find out I'd helped the djinn escape. But I remembered the power that swept over me from the master vampire, even stronger than Killian's, and the dark magic from the warlock that crawled over my skin even when he just stood still, as he was doing now.

This is what I felt when I got out of the car, and how I knew they were there before I found them.

My blood turned to ice in my veins, and I started to tremble. This wasn't good. Closing my eyes, all I could think about was Jamal, my angry vampire. I wondered if he really had the death wish he claimed, or if he just talked smack. But I guess it didn't really matter. We were both doomed now.

I'm sorry.

I'm so sorry.

Jamal...

Somehow, I forced myself to take a step forward. And then another. And another. At the entrance to the circle, I paused, but just for a second, before I stepped into it. My breath left my lungs as I felt it close behind me. There was silence from the witches around me. The only sounds from the bugs and frogs in the swamp surrounding us, along with the occasional splash of water as something slithered into it.

"She had no choice."

I jumped when the words rang out loud and clear, whipping my head around toward the source. He stood outside the circle, peering in at me between Alice and Talin. I vaguely noticed that Alex was missing, but the thought didn't hold my attention for long. I had other things to worry about. "Mike, don't," I told him.

"No." He shook his head. "Fuck that. This is bullshit." He tried to break through the circle to get to me, but the force of the witch's combined magic held him at bay. "What's happening?" he asked me when he couldn't get through. "What are they going to do?"

"Nothing more than I deserve." I dismissed my friend and looked straight at my aunt. The high priestess stared back at me with no emotion on her kind face. "So, you know."

"We know," she said, not unkindly. But the warmth she normally exuded wasn't there.

"I'd like to explain," I told her. "I know it won't change anything, but I'd still appreciate the chance to let you know what happened."

Aunt Judy glanced around the circle at everyone in turn. I was afraid to follow her gaze. I haven't always been the nicest person to many of them. More like that cousin nobody liked but everyone put up with just because they were family. But she must've gotten their approval, for she gave me a nod. "Go ahead. I'd like to hear it from your own lips. Hear how you could betray your family, your coven. How you could endanger us and our friends."

"Friends" was pushing it a bit. More than a bit. Until very recently, my aunt had tolerated the vampires in our city, and barely at that. The words were on the tip of my tongue, but for once I managed to keep my mouth shut.

"Well," she told me. "Go on. We're all very anxious to hear."

It took me a while. I had to stop and start a lot, my emotions getting the better of me at times. But eventually, I told her the entire story I'd told Lizzy, including how I helped the djinn get away from the warlock, Jesse.

The raven croaked at me, flapping her wings until Jesse soothed her with a few words and a hand over her pitch-black feathers. She settled but continued to click her beak every once in a while.

When I finished, I looked around at my coven. My family. All of the fear and anxiety I'd been living with all of this time overwhelmed me and I fell to my knees before them and begged their forgiveness, over and over, until I had no more words and I was just a trembling pile of flesh and bones kneeling in the dirt. My entire being longed for Jamal, cried out for him. Not that he would be able to save me. But maybe I'd get the chance to say goodbye and beg him to forgive me also.

"What is your decision, Judy?"

I looked up to find Jesse staring down at me. Unlike my aunt, there was nothing in his golden eyes but disgust.

When my aunt didn't answer, he offered one for her. "She deserves death."

"That's a harsh decision, warlock, and it's not up to us to make it," Luukas spoke up.

Jesse wouldn't look at him, his entire focus was on me, and it was the most terrifying thing I'd ever experienced.

"The vampire is right." My aunt finally stood up to the warlock. The woman had guts, I had to give her that. "As Luukas said, this is not your decision to make," she told him. "It's mine. My coven's. I invited you and Luukas here as a courtesy, to witness her punishment. That's it. So kindly step back and remember your place here."

I held my breath, worried for my aunt. But Jesse only smiled at her and went back to stand by Shea.

"Aunt Judy--"

With the slightest movement of her hand, she silenced me. "No," she told me. "You've said all I needed to hear." Glancing behind her at Keira, she said, "As you're family, would you join us, please?" Keira stepped up to take a place beside her, her expression carefully blank.

The slight didn't go unnoticed by me or any of the others. But Jesse only smiled and pulled Shea up against him when she shot him an anxious look.

However, it was Keira who said, "Jesse deserves to be here just as much as I do, if not more so. He's family, and if it wasn't for him, your Alex would be dead right now."

After a long silence, Aunt Judy nodded her head.

Once everyone was in the circle, they joined hands and my aunt delivered her decision. A decision, she said, that had already been discussed at length between all of the magical powers present. A decision it broke her heart to give, but one that had to be made.

For the crimes I'd committed against the coven, crimes that had used my magic to put other's lives in danger, there was really only one way this could go. There was no other way to break the bond between me and the djinn.

This would end in my death.

"No! No! You can't do this!"

Mike's scream came at me as though through a void. Even though I'd expected it, to hear the words come out of her mouth stole the breath from my lungs. And yet, other than that first shock of surprise, I just felt numb. I heard a noise to my left and looked up to find Alice crying. The rest of the coven just looked angry. And I couldn't blame them.

I got to my feet, and my eyes met those of my aunt. "Can you help Mike?" I asked her.

"Once the bond is broken between you and the djinn, we'll do what we can to protect him."

That was really all I could ask.

Jamal's sharp features floated in front of me like a mirage. I wished I'd had more time with him. More time to get to know him. To ease his fears. To love him...

I'm sorry...

Jesse suddenly cocked his head. "Someone is coming." With a softly spoken word to the raven, she flapped her wings and flew off. Everyone watched her go except for me and Mike. His eyes never left me.

I tried to give him a reassuring smile, but I couldn't.

However, I still had one play to make. The chances were pretty damn low, but maybe--just maybe--I'd be able to walk out of here with my life.

And in the process, save Jamal's.

24

JAMAL

When we drove onto the clearing where the coven was holding Angel accountable for her actions, we found her standing in the middle of a circle of witch's, all in normal street clothes, much like they'd done when they saved Kenya and when they'd performed the location spell at Lizzy's store.

This time though, the only light was from a small fire, and the way the flames darkened her eyes and danced across her white skin and red hair made her look like a demon that had just risen from the depths of hell, surrounded by the ones who wished to persecute her.

A hell it looked like I'm gonna return to with her. Because I had some revelations in the forty minutes it took us to get here. And I had some shit I needed to work out. But I got to thinking that maybe I'd like to do that with her. But first, I had to stop whatever the fuck was happening right now.

We were still probably a good quarter mile from this clearing when I felt it--magical vibrations in the air. Some darker than others, but all filled with malice, and all aimed directly at Angel. At my...

Mate.

MY mate.

All logical thought left me as soon as Alex whipped the Jeep around. Before it even came to a full stop, I was out and rushing the witches, driven purely by instinct. The only thing that slowed me down was the ring of magic surrounding them. But that's all it did--slow me down. It didn't stop me.

With a roar of pure rage, I busted through, the witches on either side of me stumbling into the others. They didn't see me coming. They had no time to move out of the way even if they were so inclined. I was in the middle of the circle, crouched over Angel's body before anyone knew what happened. Including myself.

Someone stepped toward us, and in my red-hazed vision I could only tell they were female. It made no difference to me. No one was going to hurt my mate. Gathering Angel closer to me, I zeroed in on this threat and bared my fangs, hissing in warning.

"Stop! Don't move!"

This was a voice I didn't recognize. My eyes darted around the group, trying to recognize the source. Power lashed out at the circle, stronger than I'd ever felt before. So strong I started to inch Angel and myself back toward the fire. Within the flames seemed like a safer place to be. A male appeared before me, squatted down on his haunches so we were face to face. He was a vampire. A master. But not my master.

I bared my fangs.

"Jamal, right?"

I studied him. Dark hair. Gray eyes. And something within those eyes. Something that spoke to me. Like he understood the crazy going on in my head right now. Like he lived there, too.

Still a threat. "MINE," I told him, tightening my hold on my witch.

He cocked his head, then he stood. "You didn't tell me this witch was mated to a vampire."

"I didn't know," the high priestess told him. They were all staring at us.

"You can't kill her."

Through the roaring in my ears, this voice came through. Kenya. My friend.

"You can't kill her," she repeated. "If you kill her, you kill him."

"I'm well aware," the high priestess said.

The gray-eyed vampire crossed his arms over his chest. "I assume this is one of Killian's vampires?" He paused. Someone must have confirmed it, for then he continued, "I gave him my word none of his own would be harmed. The witch stays alive and everyone...everyone," he emphasized, "needs to. Back. The fuck. Up."

As the circle around us widened, I was able to suck some air into my lungs again and my vision began to clear. But I was still afraid to move away from the witch beneath me. I didn't trust the situation. Didn't trust the vampire.

However, once everyone had given us some space, he grabbed the dark-haired witch and did the same, keeping her slightly behind him.

"Jamal, let me up."

A low growl rumbling through my throat was my only response as I kept an eye on everyone, especially the male with the bird on his shoulder who was staring at my witch with glowing golden eyes. But I did loosen my hold on her just a bit.

My mate's face appeared in front of me in the firelight, blocking out everyone else. Her soft palms cupped my cheeks, and I flashed my fangs when I saw the tears on her face. "What I did was wrong, and it threatened the life of my coven. And your friend..." Her voice broke as she glanced to her right, but I didn't take my eyes from her.

Gradually, coherent thought and speech returned, and the rage that boiled over cooled down to a simmer. I was still ready to throw down in a moment's notice, my instincts on high alert, but at least now I could talk like a normal male. "You can't die on me, Leeloo."

Her eyes shot to mine when I called her by her nickname. A smile turned up the corners of her red lips. "You're back."

"Sort of," I told her. Taking her hand, I pulled her to her feet. It didn't escape my notice that she held my eyes the entire time, keeping my attention on her. "I'm sorry." I paused, trying to figure out how to put everything I'd been going through into words. "I'm sorry I rejected you like I did. You didn't deserve to get caught up in my drama."

"Well, in case you haven't noticed, I apparently kind of like drama." Her grin was self-depreciating.

"Angel."

My head whipped up as the high priestess stepped forward. But Angel placed her palm against my chest, the gesture both soothing and a barrier. "Let me handle this," she told me. "Please."

After a moment, I gave her a nod, but I didn't move from my protective position.

"I'd like to offer you a deal," she told her aunt.

"I don't think that's--"

"I have this." Leeloo pulled something from the back of her jeans. The dagger. "I was trying to spell it to give it enough power to kill the djinn. That's what I was doing the night he found me in the graveyard. The night Jamal saved me."

She held it out to her aunt, and she approached her slowly, keeping a wary eye on me. I managed not to growl at her. "Where did you get this?" she asked her once she had the dagger in her hand.

"I took it from Lizzy's store. From the back room."

"And does it work?"

"Not quite. I managed to injure him, but that's all." She paused. "I'll hand it over peacefully, if you revoke your previous decision, and let me live. Let us live," she corrected. "And let me remain a member of the coven."

"There still needs to be consequences."

"I know," Angel told her. "And I'm good with that." Her pulse was erratic and her heart was pounding hard, but she held her ground.

She made me proud. More proud than I was of myself at this moment and my behavior up until now.

Judy studied her for a long time. "Your magic will be bound, and you're no longer a member of this coven."

Angel made a sound of distress, her hand fisting in my shirt.

"For now," Judy told her. "For now."

Angel bowed her head, sorrow and regret flowing from her to me as though we shared the same brain network. She sniffed, then lifted her head. "Thank you."

A soft breeze blew through the clearing, taking the tension from the air as Judy handed the dagger over to the warlock, the bird back on his shoulder. He studied it closely, turning it this way and that, then looked back at his vampire mate and gave her a nod.

The ceremony to bind Angel's magic got underway. I stood by and watched, staying within easy touching distance of my witch, despite the fact I could feel the spell crawling over my skin and raising the hair on my neck, my eyes locked on her the entire time. She took it with all of the strength and elegance I would expect from her, and despite what she did in the past, my admiration for her grew.

When it was done, and the crowd began to disperse, I held her in my arms and let her soak my shirt with her tears. By the time she pulled herself together, we were the only ones left besides Kenya and Alex, who were waiting inside the Jeep. Mike had gone with the coven. They were meeting the warlock and his mate at Lizzy's store to see what they could do to cut the tie between him and the djinn. They'd have to use the room at the back of the store, as it was under a protection spell and he wouldn't get wind of what they were doing until it was too late.

"Come home with me," I told her.

She looked up at me with watery hazel-green eyes. "Why would you want me to after what I did? To you? To everyone?"

"Because we're stuck together now and we gotta work some shit out." I softened my blunt words with a smile. "And because I need you, Leeloo. Despite it all."

"Okay."

"We'll stop at your place and grab some stuff."

A sliver of hope lit up her face. "Okay."

We made it back to my place about an hour before the sun, and I wasted no time getting both of us naked and in the shower to wash the swamp air off of us. I meant to be quick, but as soon as I had her alone with nothing between us, I couldn't keep my hands off of her. They slid along her soapy skin with no resistance, learning every fucking inch of her.

"I need to fuck you," I told her. "And then I need to feed and fuck you again."

She leaned back against me with her eyes closed against the spray of the shower as I wrapped my arms around her and squeezed, then slid one hand between her legs as the other found her breast. I slipped two fingers between her silky folds and down to her entrance and pushed them inside, her moans the best thing I've ever heard in my life. Pumping them in and out a few times, I pulled them out and slid my hand around her hip to cup one plump cheek before sliding my hand down and cupping her from behind, plunging my thumb into her ass. "This is mine, too," I told her. "And I'm gonna claim it, but not tonight."

Angel pushed back against my hand, telling me without words that she was perfectly okay with that, and my cock swelled to majorly uncomfortable levels. Sliding my hands up her torso and down both arms, I turned us so the shower spray was against my back and placed her hands on the tiles. "Brace yourself, Leeloo."

Without having to be told, she lifted one leg and set one foot on the side of the tub, and I wasted no time at all sliding inside of her. Our moans mingled as we became one, and I stilled, needing a moment. Grabbing her hips, I pulled out and thrust back in, quickly picking up the pace. Her body squeezed my cock, and her cries echoed off the walls as I penetrated her, over and over and faster and faster, until I could feel my orgasm tightening my balls and sliding up my shaft.

Baring my fangs with a low growl, I struck, sinking my fangs into the meat between her neck and shoulder.

Angel cried out, her body jerking hard and then settling into a shudder as she came. I was right behind her, the sweet spice of her blood running down my throat and her warm body spasming around me too much. It was all too much, and I hung onto her with one arm while I braced our fall to the tub with the other, my fangs and cock still inside of her.

Sitting on my heels, I held her tight against me as I licked the wound I made and hugged her close. We still had so much to talk about. So much to learn about each other. But for now, my soul was at peace.

"Thank you for saving me," she told me, her voice just above a whisper.

"I think it's you who did the saving," I countered. And as my heart stirred within my chest and something heavy and forever settled over me, I knew that's exactly what she'd done.

My Angel was going to set me free.

***

I hope you enjoyed Jamal and Angel's story! Book 4 is coming soon!

And if you haven't read the original Deathless Night story where we first meet Luukas and the rest of the vampires, along with their mates, you can start reading with **A Vampire Bewitched**.

Already read all of Deathless Night and looking for more? The Kincaid Werewolves have their own series, and you can start with **Lone Wolf's Claim**.

Check out my website **HERE** for even more books and the reading order of each series!

Thanks again for reading!

Much love,

L.E.

ABOUT THE AUTHOR

L.E. Wilson writes romance starring intense alpha males and the women who are fearless enough to love them just as they are. In her novels you'll find smoking hot scenes, a touch of suspense, some humor, a bit of gore, and multifaceted characters, all working together to combine her lifelong obsession with the paranormal and her love of romance.

Her writing career came about the usual way: on a dare from her loving husband. Little did she know just one casual suggestion would open a box of worms (or words as the case may be) that would forever change her life.

On a Personal Note:

"I love to hear from my readers! Contact me anytime at le@lewilsonauthor.com."